IN A PIG'S EYE

IN A PIG'S EYE

by

Karl Schwenke

Chelsea Green Publishing Company
Chelsea, Vermont

First Printing, March 1985

Library of Congress Cataloging in Publication Data
Schwenke, Karl
  In a pig's eye
  1. Swine - Fiction. 2. Country life - Vermont -
Fiction. I. Title.
PS3569.C5688I5 1985   813'.54   84-29289
ISBN 0-930031-00-8

for Sue

Newbury is where I live. It's a real, small town in Vermont with real, bigger-than-life people — people whom I have come, over the past fifteen years, to appreciate and love. Because I love them and respect their right to privacy, I have chosen (with a few obvious exceptions) to use ficticious names. In fact, in many cases I have taken the liberty of molding several town characters into unrecognizable, composite personas.

In this account I have not allowed *facts* to get in the way of *truths*, nor proper English to obscure the rural idiom. How else can one tell decent pig stories?

Karl Schwenke
January 1985

CONTENTS

1

———

HE CAME OUT, foretrotters first. His was the first birth I had ever seen, and unlike my new neighbors, Vern, Gideon, and Noah, I was struck dumb by the event. I was also, in a way that I had never experienced before, utterly useless.

It was a cold February afternoon when Gideon, Noah, and I came by Vern's place just as Vern's sow, Sarah, was delivering. Fearful of getting in the way, and awed by the act of procreation, I stood back as Gideon and Noah calmly went about helping Vern midwife the litter. They worked quietly and efficiently.

Next came the snout. Then came the mouth, complete with a tip of red tongue protruding. One of Vern's sensitive hands grasped the two tiny trotters, and he commenced to pull gently each time that Sarah grunted and contracted.

"She's been at it for two hours now," explained Vern tersely.

"Tired, aincha old girl?" he crooned as he patted Sarah's quivering side with his free hand. His obvious concern impressed me as I stood off in the chilly background.

The shiny, translucent membrane that covered the emerging piglet's head blurred the animal's features and flattened its ears back against its skull.

"What's the count so far?" asked Gideon as he thrust his age-spotted hands into the nearby steaming pail of water.

"This's the eighth," replied Vern as he tugged the piglet's shoulders free.

"Second litter?" asked Noah.

"Her sixth," answered Vern as he tensed for Sarah's next effort. "She's getting along," he added when Noah whistled appreciatively.

The significance of these exchanges was lost on me at the time. I had been in Vermont less than a year, and with my city hubris, I still regarded country people as insensitive rustics. But as the drama of the birth developed it was becoming clear to me that I was witnessing something more, a sense of . . . community? . . . commitment? . . . shared humanity? Whatever it was, I liked the honest, basic feel of it, and I suddenly wanted to know more.

Sarah's *huff!* broke into my reverie. She gave a convulsive heave that brought her head off the bed of shavings, and the partially emerged piglet suddenly popped out. For the moment, it lay still, its hind legs caught up against its stomach, its tail trailing alongside the umbilical cord. No sooner was it out than a bloody mass of membranous material followed, and there was a collective sigh of relief from the three midwives as they recognized the afterbirth that signalled an end to the procedure.

Deftly, Gideon reached across Vern's shoulder and

snipped the umbilical cord so that it hung about five inches below the baby's belly. Moving quickly, Vern cleared the tiny piglet's face and mouth of the membranous sack and then pumped its back legs back and forth.

Until then, I hadn't realized that, like the baby pig, I had been holding my breath. It came as a relief when both of our lungs sucked in life-giving air. With his first supply of breath, the piglet serenaded us with a feeble squeal. Sarah's big head rose to the sound but then fell back weakly as Vern patted her reassuringly.

Noah took the tiny squealer by the hind legs and dipped the recently severed umbilical cord into a bottle of iodine. "Nice long bacons," he observed as he deposited the new arrival alongside his siblings under a heat lamp.

"Ow!" he yelped as he suddenly jerked back a hand that showed a spot of blood welling up from a minor puncture on his index finger. "Thet leedle bugger's goin' t'be a caution when he gets of a size," he added ruefully, as he upended the iodine bottle on his finger.

"Sorry about that, Noah," said Vern. "I'll clip those sharp teeth later."

"What'd y'expect, thanks?" asked Gideon. "How'd you feel'f some fellers pulled you outen a nice warm place, give you arty-fish-uwal respiration, and tole you thet you was aimed fer the pot?"

The rest of the day's events recede in my mind. As I recall, we cleaned up the pen and went inside Vern's kitchen for some cold, hard cider. What remains vivid in my mind is a husbandryman's empathy and the miracle of that birth. They will forever remain landmarks in my rural odyssey, an odyssey that has become a quest for understanding of the rural idiom, and of myself. The quest still goes on, but as Gideon might have phrased it, "I'm gainin' on it."

2

"WE REGARD PIGS as a learning experience," said the headmaster to Sue and me as the two miniature battleships huffed by.

It was two years before the experiences in Vern's barn, and I was not yet acquainted with the profundities of the rural experience. Looking back, I regret the fifteen years it has taken to absorb what the headmaster had to say. The fact is, compared to pigs, we humans are unforgivably slow to learn from pragmatic experience.

The three of us were so bemused by the appearance of the huge hogs, we were nearly overrun by the flotilla of yelling teenagers that appeared in their wake.

"They got out again, Mister Mister!" chortled a black kid in the vanguard.

"Don't run them! They'll have a heart attack!" hollered the headmaster to the unheeding student body. Turning back to Sue and me he apologized, "I'm sorry, I'm afraid that I'll have to help round them up." At the bend in the road he paused to add, "We'd be happy to have you stay in one of our campus cabins. You might give it some thought." His Cheshire grin remained after he had gone.

Looking for a place for me to hole up for a winter of writing solitude, my wife, Sue, and I had pulled our VW bus into the dooryard (a peculiar term that Vermonters use to describe their driveways) of a generous, white clapboarded house outside Vershire, Vermont, and engaged the affable, largish man who emerged from the house in conversation. He turned out to be the owner and headmaster of a private rural school whose buildings were hidden back in the sugar bush on the other side of the road.

Whether it was our nesting instinct after a nomadic summer, Mister Mister's Cheshire grin, or just curiosity about the fate of the pigs, we quickly agreed to give the accomodations a try and followed the excited chatter of the pig chase. When we got to the main highway at the end of the drive, we were just in time for our first lesson in pig nomenclature and behavior.

The first thing we city-bred Californians learned was the difference between a pig and a hog. The closer I got, the more impressed I was with their size. The nearest was an enormous white Yorkshire boar with the typical upraised ears and long, bacon-producing profile. He was big! As I walked toward him, I realized, with some trepidation, that he outweighed me by a good half ton. Until that moment I had looked on the affair as pleasantly diversionary — a farmy interlude of herding a domestic animal back into his pen. Now I felt my first qualm.

Qualms are one thing, fear is another. It was not until the boar raised his head and looked me right in the eye that I accorded pigs the respect that they deserved. Beneath

the comical pile of black dirt on his snout curved two in-
timidating tusks. They were not terribly long, but in my
facile imagination, they grew a foot in length as I studied
them. Fearsome as these teeth were, it was the calculating
look in the periwinkle-blue eyes that claimed me. Their
innate intelligence stripped me of any false sense of hus-
bandrymanship I may have harbored.

In the brief time they had occupied the school's front
lawn, the hogs had wreaked amazing havoc. The lawn
looked as though it had been crisscrossed by a powerful
rototiller. Obeying Mister Mister's wave, I joined the excited group of youngsters in circling the animals. Looking
back with fifteen years of experience, I now know this was
the wrong thing to do. Threatened by two-legged savages,
the hogs responded with uncomfortably humanlike logic:
they "closed the circle." With rumps pressed close together
they faced outwards, transmitting through their contact
a common decision to fight or take flight.

Fortunately for us, they chose the latter. They went
through our skirmish line like Sherman through Georgia.
Now, for those who, like myself, have never seen a half
ton of pork at a flat-out run, I assure you it is an awesome
sight. Once a hog weighing twelve hundred pounds is scared
into deciding to run from point A to point C, no mere
human being wants to get in the way.

Unfortunately, Mister Mister was at point B, and they
dealt with his fifteen stone as a bowling ball does a tenpin.
To his academic credit, Mister Mister came up spitting good
Vermont dust and spouting Melville.

"Hast seen the white whale?" he shouted dazedly. "A
Quito doubloon for the white whale!"

Over the last decade, I have never made up my mind
whether it's the Vermont ambiance or merely pigs that
force pig herdsmen to revert to the classics to express

themselves properly in times of stress.

The hogs were away, sailing down the river of black-topped road like wing-on-wing yachts on parade. Undaunted by the porcine display of power, the kids were strung out behind them, and they were in full cry. Age and the consequent awareness of mortality kept the adults well to the rear. Beyond the villages, outbacker Vermonters prize their privacy, and their houses are typically spaced at comfortable quarter- or half-mile intervals. Now several hundred yards behind the pack, we watched as the hogs and the kids turned in at the neighbor's.

"We've got 'em now," screamed a frantic girl as she beckoned us on.

"Oh God," groaned Mister Mister. "That's old man Page's place. He'll raise hell about this at town meeting." What we saw when we finally arrived at the Page place reduced Mister Mister to a monotonous repetition, "Oh God . . . oh God . . . oh God."

Set back from the road, the tiny house in the clearing was surrounded by a circle of uplifted teenage bottoms. An occasional grunt sounded, and a flash of white showed between the patches of dangerously stretched denim and the low piers that supported the structure. If there were any doubts that the hogs were under the Page's house, they disappeared when the whole structure shivered as though being subjected to an earthquake.

Mister Mister covered his eyes and sat down on the blacktop with a moan. The horrendous squeal that rent the balmy fall air and the teenagers' echoes that followed left him peeking between his fingers. One of the kids had hold of a hog's tail, and despite the help of a tug-of-war line-up of two others, he was rapidly disappearing under the house.

"Let go!" gargled Mister Mister desperately. "For

Christ's sake, leggoofim!'' Finally regaining control of his
voice, the last came out in a stentorian bellow.

Startled, the boy obeyed. The slingshot effect raised
the house off its piers by a good two inches, and the hogs
burst from the other side of the crawl space as though
catapulted from the U.S.S. Enterprise. Like guided missiles,
they headed straight for a small picket-fenced enclosure adjoining the house. I assumed that it was a garden until I
saw the tombstones.

Like Juggernauts, they made matchsticks of the fence,
and then seeing no immediate pursuit (solely because of
shock), did what all hogs do when bored: they rooted.

Until that moment my brain had been chugging along
in first gear, but the moment that they entered the burial
plot, it shifted into overdrive, and the hackles on the back
of my neck rose in vague anticipation of a catastrophe in
the making. Where I hailed from, death and all its ap-
purtenances were untouchable, sacred, and spoken of only
in whispers. We hid our dead behind impregnable stone
walls and replaced the term graveyard with cemetery. My
horror at this transgression was turning my brain to jelly
when the irreverent student body let out a cry and started
for the plot.

Like a shot, the screened door of the tiny house banged
open, and old man Page emerged.

"Stop!"

It seemed impossible for the voice of God to come out
of that stooped and bent old man, but it did. Everyone
and everything stopped in a frozen tableau. Even the hogs
stopped their rooting and stood looking toward the house.

Snapping the purple suspenders that seemed to hold
his frail frame together, old man Page snorted once and
then backed slowly into the house. Except for me, the
tableau remained as it was, everyone fixated on the house.

I just knew that when he reappeared he would be carrying a shotgun, and with Sue in tow, I was inching toward the cover of a nearby popple tree.

But when he reappeared, the old man was carrying a rocking chair. He placed it in the center of the porch, sat, and put his feet up on the rail.

"Now go ahead," he boomed in that God-like voice.

*　　*　　*　　*

If I had a nickel for every time I've been asked why I came to Vermont, I'd have retired. What's so far-fetched, I answer my interrogators, about voluntarily coming to a place where the native inhabitants exhibit a xenophobia that would make a Russian communist blush? Is it so difficult, I argue, to believe that a sane person would trade the cosmopolitan polish and temperate climes of California for the rural rusticity and ball-breaking cold of Vermont?

After I have thoroughly confused the questioner, I tell him about the egalitarian nature of wayward hogs; about Mister Mister, who quotes Ahab with the same facility that he retells a joke he heard in the steamy confines of the March sugarhouse; about children who unabashedly cope with graveyards and the consequences of mortality; about Mister Page whose God-like voice hides a rock-hard sense of proportion tempered with a dry humor; and about Missus Page.

Missus Page appeared on the porch behind Mister Page's rocker and watched the goings on in the dooryard. Straight off a Norman Rockwell cover of the old *Saturday Evening Post,* she was a small, fragile woman whose snow white hair would make Bob Hope's teeth look dingy.

By this time I had sheepishly shed the comfort of my popple tree and was avidly absorbing everything about this improbable scene. Unlike that of her stoical spouse, Missus Page's face freely mirrored her emotions. Fascinated, I watched the myriad wrinkles arrange themselves into amused forbearance as Mister Mister and the student body excited the normally phlegmatic animals to an impossible frenzy as they tried to capture them.

What they would have done with a hog of this size had they been able to catch him seemed not to have occurred to anyone. Now the hogs were so skittish they would bolt at the slightest feint, so when cooler heads finally prevailed, and they attempted to herd them in the desired direction, they might as well have tried to drive the wind.

Momentarily I had taken my eyes off the porch, and when I looked back, Missus Page was gone. She reappeared in seconds, lugging a galvanized pail. My assessment of her fragility took a hitch as she came down off the porch with the grace of a woman thirty years her junior. Balancing the obviously heavy pail and contents on her hip, she marched towards the cornered hogs.

The kids made way before her hackle-raising "Sooooo-EEEEEEEpigpigpig, soooooooEEEEEEEpigpigpig, soooooo-EEEEEEEpigpigpig!" For those who have a piano, the recipe for Missus Page's hog call begins on G above middle C, and yodels into E of the next octave with the second syllable, then returns to middle C for the repetition of the next three syllables. When later I attempted to duplicate that hog call for Missus Page, she split a seam in her old print dress laughing. "You've got to get more nose into it!" she snorted.

"SoooooooEEEEEEEpigpigpig!" Her cry was as aggravating as a fingernail on a blackboard, someone chewing ice, and a naked tractor brake shoe on a brake drum, all rolled into one. It served to get everyone's attention, including the hogs'. She threw a handful of kitchen garbage in front of them, and they began to snuffle. They were wary, but finally the big boar lipped a morsel, dropped it, picked it up again, and tentatively tasted it.

From that point on it was duck soup — or whatever it was that Missus Page was canning that day. Trailing garbage behind her, she led them to the road and then passed the pail on to Mister Mister with this final thought, "Jest remember two things: pigs will always be pigs, and you don't never ketch a pig, you fetch it."

3

PIG LORE BEGINS with a situation that is dealt with by
common sense folks like Missus Page. An endless source
of fascination, pigs are responsible for poems, songs, and
nursery tales. It may even have been the nursery rhyme
extolling the industry and foresightedness of the Third Little Pig that, two years later, induced me to build a stone
house in Vermont. You remember the Third Little Pig?
He was the one giving the razzberry to the Big Bad Wolf.
It is always he who is held up as the epitome of the Christian work ethic, the paragon of permanence, while the other
two pigs are dismissed as slugabeds.

I confess to a certain smug self-righteousness while
building my stone house. Choosing Newbury as a place
to settle and build was merely happenstance, but, as it
turned out, it was a propitious choice. As other newcomers
about me — ones who had chosen to build in an easier

medium — finished their houses by summer's end, I labored doggedly on. Sweating as summer turned to fall, I thought of myself as perservering, as gutting it out, as sticking with it. "This place will stand when theirs are termite food," my ego whispered.

I remember the comments of neighbors who, late in the fall, came to check my progress. "You've got a lot of courage!" said one. "That's a clever way to put seemaynt t'gether," observed another. It pains me to think back on the look of suffering martyrdom that my face undoubtedly wore at the time. I have since come to learn that local folks use the word "courage" politely in place of simplemindedness, and that in local parlance "clever" is used by "hoss" traders to describe a sneaky and uppity draft animal.

Why is it, I wonder, that we deceive ourselves so? Worse, why is it that when we daydream or fantasize, we insist on doing it in cliches? Did the fabled Third Pig endure the same nonsense as he built to keep the Wolf from his door? Probably not, but I'll be hanged if I'll buy the traditional goody-goody ending. I prefer to think that, like me, the Third Little Pig smugly moved into his carefully crafted pile of rocks, only to endure an earth-shaking quake that same night.

For me that earthquake shook a lot more foundations than the one my house sat on. Belatedly I have realized that permanence is, at best, ephemeral. The moral of the Third Pig notwithstanding, nothing lasts indefinitely, unless it's witchgrass or pigweed (it's no accident, by the way, that pigweed is of the genus amaranth, meaning "abiding" or "everlasting"). Certainly a stone or brick house connotes a certain stability and solidity, but like all man's dreams, it too will eventually crumble to dust.

Yet seeking Third Pig permanence continues as one of man's silly preoccupations. We persist at whistling in the dark places of our minds, pleading for identity, staking a worthless claim on immortality.

It was those kinds of thoughts that were running through my head when I finished the house and took time out to meet my farming neighbors and get to know them better. Until then, farming was nothing more than a pleasant avocation, and farming people merely backdrop. When I sat in on the birthing of the baby pigs at Vern The Pig Man's place, things changed.

Our modest small-farm venture began with more enthusiasm than knowledge, and we began tentatively — with a solitary pig. That was our first mistake. We had bought our piglet from Vern, and I vividly recall his disapproval at the time of purchase. Like ourselves, Vern was a newcomer to Newbury, but he seemed to have an instant rapport with pigs — a fact I later attributed to his years of study at the Stanislavski School.

"Whuffle . . . pigs are convivialists," grunted Vern The Pig Man, "Aincha baby?" The latter was addressed to Sarah, whom he was cuddling up to. He tousled the coarse hair between her eyes and gave her a big smooch on the snout.

I have since discovered that every pig raiser is an idiosyncratic philosopher, but at the time I vacillated between the impulse to laugh or to gag. I asked, "What do you mean?"

"Whuff!" snorted Vern — he did an incredibly real imitation of an indignant pig. "Anybody, including pigs, likes company for a meal!"

The rest of the particulars of that conversation are lost somewhere in the recesses of my mind, but I do recall his contention that he could increase his pigs' food-to-weight gain by as much as 10 percent if he serenaded them at feeding time with his trumpet. At the time I attributed it to hyperbole, but when, some months later, I heard him play at a dinner party, I changed my mind. He played a mean horn, and everyone at the dinner party made pigs of themselves.

Normally not particularly politic, Vern The Pig Man kept his I-told-you-so's to a porcine squeal when I came back to buy one of my pig's siblings. As predicted, my solitary piglet spent more time pining than putting on pounds, and when he was reunited with one of his sisters, the difference in their sizes was impressive.

I had solved my pig's problem, but I had compounded my own. At the year of this writing, the average American consumes sixty-three pounds of pork each year. If you raise "feeder pigs," you usually end up with about 150 pounds of pork in the freezer for each pig butchered. Two pigs were too much for Sue and me, so we asked around and found buyers in two newcomers to town, Sal and April Burnstein.

Our troubles began when the Burnsteins' youngsters named the new pig Emily. I began to sense the danger when the family came to visit on weekends. The kids were no sooner out of the car than they were headed for the pigpen to check on Emily's well-being, and it wasn't long before the parents were joining them in making a pet out of her.

During the six months required to bring the pigs to slaughtering size, I hoped that the loss of Emily's piglet cuteness would find a corresponding lack of interest on the part of our friends. No such luck. If anything, the anthropomorphizing process intensified, and Emily became a pest.

On weekdays when the Burnsteins were not around, she took to dogging my every footstep, awaiting the least attention I might afford her. Feeding time became a trial. I discovered that Emily began to require a certain amount of personal attention — petting and a Dutch rub between her ears — before she would deign to touch the moistened grain that I put into the trough. Seeking a morsel of affection, she was forever nudging me with her rooter while I mucked out the pen or spread fresh sawdust.

A pig's rooter, or snout, is a specialized instrument. Composed mostly of bone and gristle, it is nevertheless used for the most sensitive tasks. For example, it has an amazingly accurate, built-in sensor which the pig employs to test the boards that make up its pen. Using its rooter, any pig can detect the slightest cellular flaw in the ligneous structure of a two-by-six with lightninglike rapidity. At this point the function of the rooter changes, and it becomes a battering ram.

But more about the fascinating functions of a pig's rooter later. "Emily's nudge," as we came to call it, was annoying but playful while she was a piglet. This changed when she passed the weight of a smaller linebacker from the National Football League. I vividly recall the fall weekend when the Burnsteins came for their last cloying visit. They had just returned from a downcountry trip and arrived in the dooryard just as we were doing the supper dishes.

"Y'gotta see this!" exclaimed Sue from the kitchen window.

I came. I saw. I groaned. Both of us smelled of sweat and chicken manure. We had just finished a long day of homesteader toil putting the garden to bed for the winter, and the sight of Sal and his family dressed to the nines in their go-to-Boston clothes was the next to the last thing I wanted to see. Familiar with our setup, the kids led the way as the family headed for the pigpen out behind the barn. The last thing I wanted to see was those kids leaving the door to the pigpen open, so I put on a frock and headed for the barn.

I was fast, but the kids were faster. I arrived to find

the gate gaping wide open, and the doting parents encouraging the kids' pursuit of Emily. Sal in his two-piecer and April in her miniskirt both chuckled as I slammed the gate home in Emily's face and dropped the latch.

"I don't see how we could possibly make hams and bacon out of Emily," observed April mournfully. She was blissfully unaware of the fact that she had come within an inch of causing me an hour or so of incalculable mental and physical anguish to repen the pigs.

I was saved from making a smartass reply — one that I would have regretted later — by a squeal from the pen. One expects squeals from a pigpen, and I was alerted to its human origins only when there was an answering chorus from April and Sal. I turned just in time to see Emily nudge the little girl, complete with pinafore, into the water bucket, and back the little boy into the supper slops I had just put into the trough. Sal caught his elevator heel on the fence as he bounded to the rescue, and landed with his namesake in the trough.

I figured that it was because she was less acrobatic that April chose to go through the gate. It was not until she bent to retrieve her pinafored daughter from the water bucket, and Emily came up behind to nose under the mini and give her one of her patented nudges, that I realized how I had misjudged April's athletic skills. She cleared the fence with a foot to spare. That leap would have done justice to an Olympic high jumper. They never came back after that.

Technically we sell our pigs live, this because the state of Vermont frowns on private folks dealing in meat. But it usually remains our lot to arrange for the slaughtering and butchering of our customers' animals. After this incident Emily's owners never turned a hair when I called to inquire as to their butchering preferences. I, on the other hand, had grown quite fond of the pig.

4

"IT'S ALL IN FUN!"

"But I don't wanna run for Hog Reeve," said Harry adamantly as he pushed the egg-stained plate away from him and ladled out four heaping teaspoonfuls of sugar onto his oatmeal. "I don't even 'member watinhell a Hog Reeve is, and if I did I wouldn't wanna be it!"

"It's just for the Bicentennial doin's," coaxed Edna, his wife. "Comeon honey, it's just a . . . a . . . ceremonial thing. Be a good sport. Just promise that you'll keep your mouth shut when Charlie nominates . . ."

"Chollie? . . . Chollie Dan'ls?" groaned Harry. "Jeez-umcrow, Edna, he's the town drunk! Watinhell kinda chance I got'f Chollie puts m'name up?"

Despite his protestations, Edna could see that she already had Harry on the hook. He had cut his teeth on town politics and was already considering his chances. She carefully hid her smile of triumph as she set the box of cornflakes before him, and thought how Jannette, her sister, would squirm with jealousy when she told her.

She clinched her case as she said, "The Whatchers've always held town offices, Harry." That plea to his genealogical pride always did the trick.

"Yeah," muttered Harry unenthusiastically. As they did with the Universal milkers in the barn, his big farmer's hands operated independently of his brain as they took a handful of cornflakes from the box and crushed them over the oatmeal and then helped themselves to another two teaspoonfuls of sugar. Absent-mindedly he drowned the glop with milk from the pitcher, spilling some on the oilcloth on the kitchen table in the process.

Harry's lack of enthusiasm stemmed from his unsuccessful bid for reelection as Town Selectman six years before. He never admitted it then or since, but not getting reelected when his opponent was a newcomer from the flatlands had stung, and now he found himself reluctant to put his shaky sense of self-worth on the line.

"Ceremonial, y'say?"

"You'll be a shooin," twittered Edna as she started to undo the rollers from her hair. She was already plotting how she would introduce the subject at the county ag agent's Home Dem meeting this afternoon, and she was oblivious to Harry's disquiet.

"Who else'll be runnin'?"

"Oh, I heard Betsy Brockman down to the IGA say that some young woman by the name of Burnstein was joshing with him about letting her husband's name be put in, but he can't —"

"Burnstein? —"

"Betsy says he's that longhair who built that little camp on the Old Starkweather Place on Tucker Hill last year."

Edna took the last roller from her hair and began fluffing
out the results.

"I dunno," said Harry around a mouthful of his
oatmeal. His eyes were cast down on the glutinous mass
as though he could read the poll results there, and the sour
expression on his face reflected the fact that he didn't like
what he read.

For the first time Edna recognized that something was
amiss. "It's just for fun Harry," she whined. Jannette's
gloating face haunted her as she poured Harry a second
cup of coffee.

*   *   *   *

"Sal, these are just honorary offices," April Burnstein
grumped as she poured maple syrup over her homemade
granola.

Sal Burnstein was finishing his second cup of ersatz coffee and frowning. "It's just asking for trouble," he said softly. He knew his wife's disdain for the rustic natives, and
being of gentle bent he did not share her propensity for
the politics of confrontation. "The locals would flip their
wigs!"

"Let them! It's time this town woke up to the twen-
tieth century."

"That may be, but the xenophobia is already thick
enough around this place to cut with a knife." Sal sat staring out the unfinished window of the large house that they
were in the process of restoring and pulled reflectively on
his lower lip. "I dunno," he concluded dubiously, and
lapsed into a stubborn silence.

April recognized the signs. When Sal clammed up and

picked at his lower lip, he was not to be swayed. She began to make independent plans.

*   *   *   *

It was all in fun. The Bicentennial town meeting was a mock affair conceived by the local Bicentennial committee more for the benefit of the anticipated influx of tourists than for the local populace. Seth Thomas presided as Moderator. Bedecked in knee britches, silk stockings, and a tri-corner hat, he briskly conducted the early part of the meeting as he conceived proper for a 1776 affair.

All went smoothly until he asked, "Do I hear nominations for the office of Hog Reeve?"

"I nominate Harry Whatchah," rasped Charlie Daniels. There was a titter amongst the knowing in the audience, and Charlie's nearest neighbors flinched as his whiskey-laden breath assaulted them.

"Seconded!" The latter came swiftly and incisively from Parsee Parsons. Everyone grinned. No one ever beat Parsee to a "second" or an "I so move." It took the newcomer several meetings to know that the birdlike little man's clipped "seconds" and "moves" were limited to just that. Though he was always perched attentively on the edge of his bench and appeared to follow the proceedings avidly, he was never once known to participate beyond that.

"I nominate Karl Schwenke." It was my friend Vern. I found myself blushing unaccountably. His nomination was unexpected, and I suddenly realized that this was the first time in my life I had ever been proposed for any public office.

"Seconded!" piped Parsee.

"I nominate April Burnstein." The nominator was a young, long-haired woman whose demeanor and dress proclaimed her one of the newcomer, alternative culture types.

"Damned huppies," muttered the middle-aged, crew-cut man next to me. His dislike was obvious, and his audible moan nearly drowned out Parsee's automatic second and the chorus of "Who's she?"

Seth cast a quick look of interrogation at Mabel, the Town Clerk. "I'm sorry miss . . ." he said finally.

"Miz," corrected the young woman staunchly. "Miz Mary Roberts."

"Mizzzzzz . . . Roberts," mimicked Seth milking the road crew types who always stood in the back for a laugh. "I'm afraid that I don't know you. Are you a registered voter in this town?"

"Yes," replied the woman shortly.

"And so am I," added April Burnstein as she stood and faced the gathering. "My name is April Burnstein, and I moved here a year ago." She paused to make careful eye contact with the hundred or so people. There was a tangible and mounting sense of dislike in the room that seemed accentuated by the buzzing of a heat-activated fly against the sunny window. "I think that it's important for women to hold public office . . . even if it's merely a ceremonial position . . . and so I welcome this candidacy." With that short speech she sat down, and a heavy silence ensued.

Discomfited, Seth cleared his throat and then asked, "Are there any further nominations?" Silence. "Do I hear a motion that nominations cease?"

"So moved," piped Parsee.

"All those in favor say aye." There was a muffled, indistinct response.

"Those opposed?" Silence.

"I hereby declare nominations for Hog Reeve closed,"

intoned Seth mechanically.

"Mr. Moderator . . ."

"Yes, Mr. Whatcher."

"I want to thank Cholly Dan'ls, but I wish to remove my name from consideration for this job. Let's leave Hog Reevin' for the flatlanders."

Seth pounded his gavel to silence the harsh laughter. An old hand at moderating these meetings, he sensed an edge to the meeting, and he attempted to back-and-fill.

"All right Harry. But the office of Hog Reeve should not be treated lightly. It is the responsibility of the Hog Reeve to act in a quasi-judicial fashion to settle disputes arising from errant swine." Having delivered himself of the description he had read the night before in an account in the town history, he continued, "We have two names for the office of Hog Reeve. Are you ready for the vote?"

"Just a minute Seth!" Edna Whatcher rose to her feet. "Aren't we pretendin' that this is a town meeting in 1776?"

"Yeah," replied Seth suspiciously.

"Then women can't hold office." Having dropped her bombshell, Edna settled back in her seat with a look of prim satisfaction on her face.

For five minutes the meeting dissolved into a gabbling mass of disputatiousness, and hurried, whispered consultations on the podium. Looking appropriately harrassed, Seth finally gavelled for silence and said, "It appears that Mrs. Whatcher is correct . . . " Commotion around the room. ". . . however, at this point The Chair rules that we vote on the issue."

"That ain't accordin' t'the rules!" shouted Charlie Daniels.

"Ahhhshuddup Charlie!" said Seth disgustedly. "This is a genuine women's liberation issue, and it's only fair that we vote on it. Do we have any discussion?"

Her face black with frustration, April Burnstein shot to her feet. "No right to hold public office? . . . that's an outrage! I —"

"You shouldn't never've been given the vote anyways!" came an anonymous catcall from the area of the road crew. As a group they all hid huge grins behind upraised hands.

"I'll have order!" boomed Seth. His robust baritone voice was an unlikely one for a village storekeeper. "You boys want to say something, then you raise your hands! Go ahead Miz Burnstein."

Ignoring Sal's tugging at her hand, April sputtered, "Women have earned the right to vote and hold office by the skin off their knees. They've —"

"Sssssss," came the sibilance from another quarter of the room.

Tears of frustration clouded her eyes as she lashed back, "You are a bunch of snotty-nosed hic —" At this point Sal managed to haul her down to her seat.

He rose and said calmly, "I call for the question."

"Seconded," squeaked Parsee.

"Okay," said Seth ignoring the unnecessary second. He was determined to get over the unpleasantness. "Here's the question. Should women . . . in this year of 1776 . . . be allowed to hold public office. All those in favor will signify by saying aye."

The hall shook with the answering "aye!"

"All those opposed will signify by saying no."

Again the hall shook. It sounded to me as though the noes had it, but I was seated near the back, and the road crew voted as a man.

"The Chair cannot determine the count, so we will have a division of the house." Seth had to raise his voice to be heard over the buzz of conversation and laughter. "All those in favor of the motion will stand to my right, and all those opposed will stand to my left!"

The town sorted itself out.

My heart fell as I watched a general rush to Seth's left. Sue and I rose and made our way to his right. I reminded myself that it was all pretend as I turned to face my fellow townspeople on the other side of the hall. At this point I discovered they had forgotten that this was not for real. The noes were a grim-faced lot. I glanced about me at my fellow ayes, and found them to be a mirror of the other side, albeit younger.

The count was interminable. Finally Seth motioned everyone to resume their seats and then announced the results. "The count is fifty-three noes, and forty-seven ayes. The noes have it, and women, in this year of 1776, are hereby denied the right to hold public office."

There followed an isolated cheer, but for the most part there was a stony silence as Seth continued, "You have also, by default, elected Karl Schwenke to the office of Hog Reeve."

The fun was gone from my day.

* * * *

Honorary title or not, it was my first public office. Seth's description of the Hog Reeve's duties had been sketchy, and I resolved to delve deeper when I got home.

My library yielded only one source, an early historical account of the goings on in the nearby town of Chelsea, Vermont. It contained two references to the office of Hog Reeve. The office was a common one to most old Vermont towns, and the first reference verified Seth's job description; the second item demonstrated the kinds of pigheadedness that a Hog Reeve had to deal with. The account caused me to celebrate the honorary nature of my new office.

In 1809, Chelseans had settled into a comfortable religious rut. The Congregationalists' Reverend Nobles was one of those quiet, dignified kinds of ministers. He had enjoyed two years of peaceful, uncomplicated pastorship when the rival preacher, the Reverend Fredrick Plummer, moved into town. Plummer was a different kettle of fish. Brash, dynamic, and filled with an alternative Christian zeal, he proselytized at a rate that would make a modern-day Mormon missionary green with envy. In the space of one year he accumulated a flock of diehards that could outamen, outsing, and outhallelujah any strait-laced Calvinist Congregationalist in town. It was a sectarian repeat of the rivalry between Vermont's loudmouthed Green Mountain Boys and the staid Royalist Tories.

Obviously such dissention could not go on untested for long, and in 1811 when the Congregationalists met and decided to build a church, matters came to a head. The choice for a building site was on Post Office Street, one of the four streets bounding the town common. Josiah Darah lived next door to the proposed building site, and as a rabid anti-Congregationalist he vociferously opposed the project.

What has all this to do with the office of Hog Reeve, you might well ask. At this point I was asking myself the same question, but I was not long in coming by the answer. The town meetings were knock-down, drag-out affairs, and having just come from one, I could well understand the petty wrangling that must have surrounded the proposed new church.

Finally the construction was begun. One by one, all the pettifogging roadblocks that Darah could erect were dismantled. Darah made his last stand in a public meeting when he vowed, "If that church is erected there I will build a hog house right under its eaves, and put forty hogs into it! And those hogs will not have a mouthful to eat on Saturday. Come Sunday, when those people have assembled, I will go out and feed them corn . . . one ear at a time . . . for the duration of the service!"

That was where the Hog Reeve stepped in. It is a crying shame that these historic negotiations are not recorded, for whatever arguments that worthy used to convince Mr. Darah to desist seemed to have worked. One thing is sure: if that Hog Reeve were alive today, he could find productive work in places like Lebanon and divorce courts.

5

___

YOU CANNOT LIVE LONG in our town without learning a lot about pigs and, as a consequence, also learn a lot about your neighbors. Nearly everyone has, at one time or another, raised pigs. And if they have not raised pigs, they invariably have a pig story or two to tell. I'm not sure what it is about the animal, but pigs bring out the yarn spinner in the shyest of folks.

One of the first people I ever met in town was Gideon Whitman, a retired swineherd. His doleful face, arthritically crippled body, and painfully shy manner put some folks off, but once he got to know you, he was, in the local parlance, a real hand to visit. It was from Gideon that I got my first inkling of how a lifetime association with pigs inevitably affects your relationship with your fellow man. In self-defense swineherds become sociologically insightful, or they become liars. Gideon was both, and he was a neighbor.

In this part of Vermont you separate "just folks" from "neighbors" by your driving manners when you pass on back roads. You wave to folks you know, and you stop to pass the time of day with neighbors. Window to window, neighbors turn off their engines and chat. Fortunately there is little traffic on our remote roads, so a sizeable amount of visiting gets done before a dust cloud appears in your rearview mirror. Even then folks understand the custom, and there is never any disagreeable display of temper if neighbors are slow to move on — downcountry folks are a different matter.

Gideon was a great one to run the roads. He was always doing some errand or other, going "downstreet," visiting his kids, or just "cruisin'." Everyone knew his salt-eaten old Dodge pickup — he once described it to me as "a bucket of rust holdin' two bumpers together" — by its distinctive hood ornament. The decoration was a gleaming chrome pig of heroic proportions that appeared to be frozen in mid leap.

During one of our window-to-window visits I asked him about the figure, and his dour face screwed up into a gargoylish grimace that I later learned was his idea of a friendly smile as he said, "Demned truck come with an *ovis canadensis* up theyah, and thet didn't seem fittin' fer a ungulate fancier, so I swapped a hog hook fer it with a eyeron monger over t'Northfield way."

"*Ovis canadensis?*"

"Sheep."

"Ungulate?"

"Pig."

"'Eyeron monger'?"

"Whitesmith. Y'heard of a blacksmith, aincha?"

"Oh, ironmonger!"

"Yup, eyeron monger." Seeing I was hard of hearing, he raised his voice. "Yessir . . . eyeron mongers and swineherds . . . both're pretty much gone now. We're useless as tits on a boar hog."

Gideon never used English when Latin would do. When I questioned this idiosyncracy he would wax indignant and remind me that Latin is the "mothah" tongue. He once told me that he learned his Latin when he hired on to herd pigs for a Latin professor from Dartmouth. "Usta lend me books t'read on the drive from Topsham t'Bradford," he said. "I'd learn pigs all day, and Latin all night . . . Pig Latin, y'might say," he added seriously.

Because he never laughed, I was always uncertain with Gideon where the philosophical pig lore left off and the lies began. I remember when he and I volunteered, as part of a civic Memorial Day project, to mow an old overgrown graveyard on Jefferson Hill, and he told me about Newbury's famous Detective Pig. We had hand mowed for about an hour, and were pausing for a rest under an apple tree when he began.

"Didja know thet some boar pigs, when they're born, have extry-sen-sory powers in their balls?"

While working he had told me the yarn of how he had managed to shoot ten "pahtridge" with a single bullet, and I was understandably dubious. "Nope," I said, "but I hope it makes more sense than your partridge story."

His doleful face took on a martryed look as he sniffed, "Disbelievers're always the last to know, and the first in the unemployment lines."

I snorted as I pictured ten partridge keeling off the round watering tub, and the smoke curling out of Gideon's calculatedly bent rifle barrel. "Okay," I said finally, "tell me about these ESP pigs, and how do you know that they keep this marvelous power in their balls?"

"I only knowed one," said Gideon, his homely face taking on a faraway look. "It was Memorial Day back in nineteen and fifty-three. I come over t'Parsee Parsons' place t'help his sow farrow. I got there just as she started t'push the first'un. It warn't her first time t'farrow, but she was have'n a helluva time with thet first pig so I reached in and checked. Little feller was sideways." Gideon's gnarled and deformed fingers writhed as though independently recalling the blessed event.

"I got'm turned 'round in good shape, and out he popped. The little cuss wasn't breathin', so I dipped him in a bucket'f cold water. I was standin' there holdin' him by the hind legs when I says t'myself, 'How many of you are there in there?' Thet little boar reaches a trotter down and makes a mark in the sawdust . . . like this." He used the butt end of his scythe's snath to draw "VIII" in the dirt at his feet.

"Roman numerals, of course," I noted derisively. "And I guess he spoke Latin too?"

"I never thought t'ask," responded Gideon with a straight face. "But he was right about about how many piglets thet sow was carryin'."

I stifled a laugh. "One could say that he was observant. But just because he knew how many brothers and sisters were left doesn't mean he had ESP."

"That's right! *Petitio principii* and *non sequitur*. That's why, after I got done with the delivery, I got down to brass tacks with thet little pig."

"What did you ask him?" I hated to admit it, but he had me hooked.

Gideon looked about the graveyard as though he suspected there were eavesdroppers present, and then said, "Y'know about *the murder*, doncha?"

Like everyone else in town, he lowered his voice to

a stage whisper when he said those two words. Our town's
only claim to homicidal notoriety, the Gibson case, still
provokes strong feelings, and I suddenly remembered that
Gibson had been murdered on about this same day by
assailants that still remain unknown.

"Yes," I said impatiently.

"Well suh! *The murder* had just happened, and folks
was lockin' their doors. The state troopers were flockin'
'round here with their lie detectors, and reporters was so
thick y'couldn't go t'the outhouse without oneof'm handin'
you the toilet paper. They didn't find out nothin', but . . .,"
here he paused with the built-in timing that all good
storytellers have before continuing, ". . . but that little pig
knew."

"Knew what?"

"Who dunnit, of course!"

I inhaled abruptly. It was absurd, but the question
popped out before I could stop it. "Who did he say done
. . . did . . . it?"

"Don't hurry me," said Gideon fretfully. "Y'gotta get
an understandin' of pig farrowin' b'fore y'get the whole
picture. I only had time t'ask a couple a questions of this
smart one b'fore the rest of his brothers and sisters came
along and took up my attention." He tugged at the peak
of his striped engineer's cap with the effort at remembering. "I remember askin' him how many people were in
on the murder, and he wrote . . . ." The snath traced an
"I" and a "V" in the dirt. "Then I asked him what time
in the mornin' did the murder take place. That little critter was smarter'n a whip. He took that little trotter of his
and wrote . . . ." He scratched out a "V".

"Then what did you ask?" I prompted.

"That was when the sow got busy," he replied. "Parsee
come along 'bout that time, and it got kind of hectic for

the next hour while she dropped the other seven. When we was cleanin' up the afterbirth, Parsee said that he wanted t'clip their eye teeth and give'm their shots right off, so I went out t'my truck t'get my gear. By the time I got back Parsee'd made barrows outa every demned one'f those baby boars."

I groaned as I anticipated the end to the story. "So when you lifted the pig up and asked him who committed the murder he didn't do anything, right? He'd lost his ESP with his balls?"

"Well, I wouldn't exactly say that," hedged Gideon.

"What do you mean?"

"I asked him the question, and he used his trotter jest like b'fore."

"And?"

"What he wrote didn't make no sense. Here . . . see . . . it looked like this . . ." He smoothed the ground with his boot and scratched the message, "U . . . S.O.B.!"

6

This little pig went to market.
This little pig stayed home.
This little pig had roast beef.
This little pig had none.
And this little pig went wee, wee, wee,
   all the way home.

WE HAVE ALL RECITED the nursery rhyme to a baby's toes. It is one of those Mother Goose things that is so bad that it has to have some deep, ponderous significance. I suspect that I am overreacting, but the big toe line, "This little pig went to market," always makes me cry, for it conjures up my first pig-loading experience.

It had been a rainy fall, and the pigs' pen and the three pigs we had raised in our expanding pig venture were a mess. Their twelve pointed little hooves had churned the mud into a quagmire that swamped our calf-high rubber boots, and made mucking out an impossibility. We had heard dire tales of the woes of loading pigs, but we still weren't ready for the reality. We had decided that the mornings, when the mud had hardened somewhat in the colder temperatures, would be the best time for the undertaking.

If you raise pigs you soon learn that there is always an abundance of advice about loading pigs, but little hands-on help. Among the more logical suggestions we received was one from our mailman, Charlie Daniels. His idea was that we build a loading ramp to the back of our covered pickup and park the vehicle at the pen the night before with the foot of the ramp available to the pigs. This, we decided, was one of Charlie's ideas that didn't come from the bottom of the bottle of Old Crow that he carried on his star route. It made sober sense. That alone should have warned us.

We made an early morning appointment with the slaughterhouse and started our preparations that very afternoon. Unfortunately the only way to get the pickup to the pen was to back down through a muddy field, where we promptly got ourselves mired to the axles. While we were standing about kicking at the mud and pondering how to get ourselves out, Charlie's mud-spattered Plymouth topped the small rise on the town road adjoining the field. It was late enough in the afternoon for Charlie to have finished his route, and I knew that he would be well down towards the bottom of the pint of Old Crow. The Plymouth made a fishtailing halt at our driveway, and Charlie emerged.

"Thet truck was meant for t'drive on top of the ground, not under it," he hollered.

"Thanks, Charlie," said Sue witheringly.

Her sarcasm lost to Old Crow. "How about stopping by Whatcher's place and asking Harry to bring his tractor down to pull us out?" I shouted back.

"No need'a thet," said Charlie opening the Plymouth's trunk. "This otta do the trick." He drew out a four-foot Handyman tractor jack. "Gotta couple a planks?"

I was dubious, but somehow Charlie's plans always verged on being sensible. "I guess so," I replied and slogged through the mud to a pile of old lumber left over from building the house. I found two mildewed two-by-tens, and lugged them over to the pickup. While I was gone, Charlie had weaved through the mud and set the jack up under the truck's rear bumper. Before I could set the old lumber down he had the wheels clear of the muck.

"Slideum under," instructed Charlie confidently.

I did as told.

"Nawthin' to it," crowed Charlie as he released the jack.

The sodden crunch of the planks as they sagged under the weight of the truck barely gave me time to fall backwards into the mud. When the planks finally broke, the nearest swivelled in the mire and put a six inch crease in the rear fender. Meanwhile, the jack slipped forward, was caught between the descending bumper and the tailgate, and was driven solidly into the water-impregnated ground. I moaned when I saw the dent the jack had made in the truck's tailgate.

Charlie stood looking disconsolately at his buried jack. "Reckon I'll fetch Harry Whatcher'n his tractor," he said finally.

Harry's good natured jibes came with his sixty-five horsepower Case tractor, and Sue and I managed the proper amount of stoicism. It was dark before we got the truck and ramp into place. Neighborliness forbade Harry from taking anything for the help, but the unofficial Vermont scales of favors were now heavily tilted in his favor. I knew that I would have to pay in kind, and custom decreed that the payment be generous.

Charlie's parting advice was to bait the trap and to have a piece of plywood handy to close off the escape route when we came down to check the results in the morning. At this point I had developed a certain amount of what I regarded as well-deserved cynicism for Charlie's advice, but having gone this far, I decided to go whole hog. Rummaging around I found a piece of plywood that would effectively close off the end of the truck bed and left it handy. Then I larded the pickup bed with broken squash, a pig delicacy, and upped the ante with a sackful of partially frozen wild apples. The pigs were already curious, so to titilate them further, I left a handful of the apples on the ramp.

It was still dark, but a faint light was creeping up over Leighton Hill the following morning when Sue and I approached the truck on tiptoe. A snuffle from inside the pickup heartened us, but our hopes took a downturn as we made out one of the pigs lying on the ramp. There were no other pigs in sight, so we assumed that the other two were sleeping off the feast inside the truck.

That left only the sentry on the ramp. I looked closely and discerned that his head was uphill, pointed toward the truck interior. I grinned as I recalled that I had purposefully narrowed the ramp so that it would accomodate only one pig at a time. I motioned Sue toward the plywood, and she nodded understanding. When she was in position to slide the improvised door home, I vaulted the fence and charged the ramp with a yell.

The sentry woke with a trumpeting squeal. He made one step up the ramp, shied away from the sight of Sue, and somehow levitated himself high enough so that he could make a 180-degree turn. Unfortunately I was halfway up the ramp when he charged. He got his snout between my knees and rooted me over the rails of the ramp. I landed with enough force to break the frozen crust of the mire. As I lay there, partially submerged in the smelly muck, I made the one fatal mistake common to all beginning pig loaders — I allowed the issue to become personal. It was now a matter of principle!

Using her head, Sue shoved the plywood across, and we had two pigs safely in the truck. I shook off the worst of the mud and picked up a hoe that we kept handy for cleaning out the pig's trough.

"Alright you bastard," I raged, "move!" I thrust the wooden end at his lowered head. He promptly bit the end of the hoe off, and stood there chewing it thoughtfully.

That action sobered me.

"I think," observed Sue in the morning gloom, "that we better have a conference."

I climbed wearily over the fence, and Sue stood upwind. "What do you suggest?" I asked.

"The feed bucket?"

"I guess it's worth a try," I agreed. We had never tried it, but we had heard that if you got the pig to eat some grain from a bucket, you could jam the bucket over the pig's head, and it would back up reflexively. With a second person to guide the rear of the pig by simply tugging on its tail, the pig could be backed up a ramp into the loading vehicle.

*   *   *   *

By the time we located a bucket big enough to cover the boar's head, the sun was up and the muddy surface in the pen had begun to melt. The pig eyed us warily as we approached bearing grain.

He looked bigger in the full of the sun.

Trying to appear nonchalant, Sue waded through the mud on my right, and I began murmuring sweet nothings as I rattled the grain in the bucket and held it low so that the pig could see the contents.

"SooooooEEEEEEEpigpigpig," I crooned. "Put your miserable little head in my bucketpigpigpig."

Whatever the merits of this technique, there was no room for human dignity. Ten minutes of backing the pig around the pen finally began to show results as he took longer each time before he spooked. He was leery of Sue's form always circling on his flank, but at last he took a tentative taste of the grain. I felt like the trout fisherman who, feeling the gentlest of tugs on his line, waits, heart in mouth, to be sure before setting the hook.

Wham! I crammed the sugaring bucket full onto his head and knew instantly that I had all I could handle — if not more. He gave a mighty squeal. He bucked. He sunfished. He jumped. He backed.

"Grab his tail," I croaked, desperately hanging on.

"I'm trying," she bit off breathlessly, and she was. Twice she got hold of that muddy, six-inch tassel only to have it slip away. Each time she ended up sprawled on her back in the mire.

The fourth time we came round the pen she got the knack of it, and before the enraged boar knew it, he was part way up the ramp.

"Quick! Move the plywood!" I shouted, and I had immediate cause to wish I could take the words back. As she released the tail to grab the plywood, the boar sensed that he was free, and he redoubled his fishtailing moves. I was barely holding my own when, to my horror, I beheld the two now freed pigs coming to their brother's aid.

Strange thoughts cross your mind at moments like this. The only thing that kept me from bailing out at that moment was my ego. I fantasized the degrading caption our local weekly would use to cover the story "Prominent Person Pummelled by Pigs."

With a superhuman effort, I gained another foot, but I knew that I wouldn't last much longer. "Do something!" I screamed above the cacophony of angry squeals.

To Sue's credit, she dithered only briefly before taking positive action. She jumped down, scrambled to the front of the truck, and leaned on the horn.

That is not what I would have done.

Which goes to show you what I knew about pigs. I am now a firm believer in feminine intuition. At the blat of the horn, all three pigs froze with their snouts up and their eyes rolled back in the direction of this new threat. It was all I needed. I made one last push, and their tiny hooves slid backwards on the slick metal. I slammed the plywood in their faces and collapsed laughing on the ramp.

We were exhausted but determined to secure the ground that we had gained at such expense. Wedging the plywood in place, I slammed the tailgate home. It was so badly dented from the jack fiasco the day before that it refused to latch, and it took our combined strengths to force the locking bolts into place. With the pigs contained, we set about getting the pickup across the field without getting stuck again.

The additional weight of the pigs on the rear of the truck and the residual morning frost on the ground did the trick. We made the trip without so much as a slip of the wheels. Parking the truck in the dooryard, we dragged our battered bodies onto the porch where we deposited our filthy clothes and raced each other for the first shower.

An early morning fog had settled into our valley by the time we had finished our ablutions and eaten a hearty breakfast, but the fog failed to dim our bright spirits. The worst was behind us, and we started for the butcher's abbatoir in uninhibited good humor. We were just passing the old Calley swamp when I glanced in the rear view mirror and watched a pig doing cartwheels.

Normally pigs don't do cartwheels.

My stomach lodged in my throat as the reality sank in, and I locked the brakes. Sue bounced off the dashboard and was sputtering the beginnings of a nasty comment as I threw open the door and dashed to the rear of the truck. There my worst fears were realized. The faulty tailgate was down, the sheet of plywood was gone, and so were the pigs.

*   *   *   *

As a respected town elder and recognized raconteur, Noah Slack is listened to, and never more so than when he tells the Cawley Swamp story. It always begins, "I was out of a mornin' surveyin' the Cawley Swamp when I first heard old man Cawley's lost voice." At this point everyone stops what they are doing to listen. From experience they know that they are to be treated to a good yarn.

"It was kinda foggy," says Noah. "A cuff-wettin' fog like we get of October. I was jest enjoyin' the sounds of the leaves fallin', and sharpenin' stakes before I set the nawtheast corner of the lot."

It should be noted here that all of us at one time or another have seen Noah Slack out on one of his solitary trips along someone's boundaries, so such tales have the smell of true fact. His knowledge of local property lines is legendary, and it was easy to visualize him hunkered down with his old square-helved axe taking measured shavings from a maple branch and dreaming up a new yarn.

"Of a sudden I heard this commotion down'n the swamp," continues Noah. "Twarn't nawthin' I ever heard b'fore. Kinda eerie'n the fawg. I listened close, and t'me it sounded like 'SoooooooEEEEEEEEE'."

"Well mistah," said Noah with a shudder, "It gave me the willies. All I could think of was old man Cawley. He's passed on now, but I 'membered the story he told me of the time he lost old Sue, the family cow. It was back in thirty-six, 'bout this same time'a year. He said that he found her tracks leadin' down into thet swamp.

"Now, old man Cawley was a God-fearin' man, but he swore thet they was sompthin' in thet place. 'Whatevah went in,' he says, 'nevah come out!' " At this point in the yarn Noah's bushy eyebrows would always crawl up his forehead, and his audience would hold its collective breath.

"Until now," Noah went on, "I nevah believed'm. 'SoooooooEEEEEEEEE,' come thet voice from the swamp. 'SoooooooEEEEEEEEE, SooooooooooEEEEEEEEE.' old man Cawley says thet he spent the best part of the day traipsin' around the swamp hollerin' fer that demned cow. He said that he shouted and shouted, until he shouted hisself hoarse. He plumb lost his voice in thet swamp, and it nevah come out! He nevah spoke a word again. Old man Cawley's voice is lost in thet swamp, still wanderin' around lookin' fer thet demned cow."

As he ends the yarn, Noah's eyebrows always make sorrowful parentheses around fierce eyes that dare the audience to disbelieve. A sharp, double-thinking listener might venture to ask how old man Cawley could have told Noah the story if he had lost his voice in the swamp. Noah will fix the sceptic with an icy glare as his eyebrows inch up into angry carets. "Only flatlanders don't know the truth when they hears it!" he will sniff disdainfully.

Unlike some doubters, I have never dared disbelieve Noah's yarn, and in return, he has never told anyone how silly a grown, angry man looks and sounds to an amused bystander when he is chasing three escaped pigs through a swamp. However, the fact that he has never told the story of how we recaptured those pigs is less a measure of the effectiveness of détente than it is a profound fear of Mabel McIndoe's displeasure.

*   *   *   *

After he got over his laughing fit, Noah joined Sue and me in the pursuit. Having a half a ton of pork on the loose is bad enough, but when an ally is decrepit and can't stop laughing, the situation becomes intolerable. At times like this you are certain that things couldn't get much worse, and then they do. Until now the pigs had led us in a straight line through uninhabited willow bogs, blackberry tangles, and uliginous mires, but they suddenly veered to the left on a crosslots course that would, I calculated, bring us out on the Scotch Hollow Road.

It did. We were strung out Indian fashion with me in the lead when we came up into Mabel and Freddy McIndoe's back yard. The pigs were nowhere in sight, and fearing the worst, we circled the house. It was as though those pigs had a built-in radar for trouble, and I knew that Mabel would be a potful. To put it kindly, Mabel is a formidable woman whose sheer bulk intimidates when her humorlessness fails — which is seldom.

Noah summed up our shared horror when he appeared

at my shoulder. "Ohmigod, they're in Mabel's flowerbeds!" he wheezed.

All but the hardiest chrysanthemums, calendulas, and violas of her prize-winning garden had been hit by the morning frosts, and those that had survived were now being methodically consumed by the pigs. They began alphabetically with the bed of calendulas, and were working into the chrysanthemums when Mabel was drawn to the front door by the ruckus. She emerged, all two hundred or so pounds of her, in predictable humor — all of it bad.

Determined to avoid sounding like a snivelly dog, I put a jocular lilt to my voice as I said, "Morning, Mabel."

"Don't 'morning' me," she snapped as she took in the scene. "Tell your pigs to get out of my flower garden!"

Turning sternly on the nearest pig who had frostbitten calendulas hanging out of both sides of her mouth, I said, "Get out of Mabel's flower garden!"

The sow finished eating the calendulas and peed on the violas.

"Fredrick!" barked Mabel over her shoulder. It was easy to see why folks called her the Sergeant behind her back. Freddy, her brother, appeared instantly, and I figured that he had been just behind the door, waiting apprehensively for her call. Old timers say that Mabel "ran Freddy something fierce when they were kids," and although they were now in their early fifties, "the habit stuck."

Aiming her tiny little eyes at her brother, she snapped, "Get those animals out of my garden!"

In the best of times it's hard to like either of the McIndoes, much less feel sorry for them, but at that moment I felt sorry for Freddy. Dwarfed physically and temperamentally by his sister, he eyed the pigs with understandable wariness. He is normally loquacious — particularly in public meetings — but now he clearly had no better ideas than we did on how to get the job done, so he did and said nothing.

The uncomfortable silence was broken only by the yapping of Mabel's miniature poodle, who was doing pogo stick jumps against the front door. I could see that Mabel was building up to another of her useless pronouncements, so I said, "If we can use your garage to hold these critters while we bring the truck around, we'll get them out of your hair."

As I spoke, the big boar found the slimy little fish pond set between the day lilies and the hollyhocks and was sucking up water as though he intended to drain it. His thirst quenched, he then meditatively waded into the water and settled down with a contented sigh.

I think that it was the sight of that boar stretched out in her fishpond that finally convinced Mabel that cooperation would accomplish more than dictums, and she gave Freddy a preemptory wave that would have done Queen Elizabeth proud at a postcoronation parade.

With Freddy's help and the use of his parked car and truck, we managed to funnel two of the pigs into the garage. The boar stubbornly refused to be moved from his mecca of mud and slime, and by consensus we left him there. Meanwhile, Sue trudged all the way back to our truck, drove it back to our place to pick up the loading ramp, and then returned.

As she backed up to the garage, I turned to Noah saying, "Noah, if you need to get back to work, I guess that we can handle it from here."

"Hah!" huffed Noah, "I wouldn't miss the end of this fer all the maple seerup in Vermont!"

Everyone except Mabel helped, and we made short work of moving the two pigs from the garage to the truck. It was deceptively easy, as our subsequent efforts to capture the boar proved. He was not to be budged from his slimy fishpond, and matters were not helped when Mabel inadvertently let her yappy little poodle loose.

After fifteen minutes of prodding with rakes and hoes we had finally shifted the boar over to the edge of the pond, and the poodle chose that moment to make dashing forays at the somnolent pig's snout, culminating in a savage attack on a floppy ear. What happened next was a blur of action. Squealing in pain, the boar threw his head back as he scrambled forward to dry ground. The poodle, refusing to give up his prize ear, was propelled over the boar's shoulder, and following a graceful half-gainer, landed in the slime.

The silence that greeted the poodle's algae-bedecked appearance as he dog paddled to dry ground was ominous. Even the boar seemed stunned by what he had done. Mabel was not. One look at her bedraggled pet and she trumpetted her charge. She swept forward, taking down the last of the calendulas in her fury, and she was on the boar before he had a chance to react.

In a movement known to wrestlers as the "gut wrench," she straddled the pig, wrapped her considerable arms around his midsection, and wrenched upward. All four trotters came off the ground at once, and in this ignominious fashion, Mabel bore the squealing boar to the truck in a rush. There she deposited him amongst his siblings with a disdainful throw, one which I am convinced she could easily have converted into a half-nelson and a pin.

"Gawd!" observed an awestruck Noah at my side, "So that's what they mean by piggyback."

As we pulled out of the McIndoe's dooryard I got to wondering what kind of agent's fee could be wangled for discovering an Olympic wrestling star of this magnitude.

7

IF YOU WERE TO ASK randomly around town, I suppose
anyone you picked could come up with a dozen reasons
why they find it hard to like Freddy or Mabel McIndoe.
Human nature being what it is, feeling warm towards the
most propertied people in town (excluding the summer
folks, of course) is just not likely. It doesn't matter that
Freddy and Mabel got where they are by exercising New
England's traditional values, frugality and thrift, or that
they are shrewd enough to recognize that the real seat of
power in town resides in the minor bureaucratic positions
of local government — Mabel having held the offices of
town treasurer and town clerk. Folks just don't seem to
like them.

But pugnacious people, like their swine counterparts,
test you, and from this testing you learn how to cope. As
a result, no occupation I have been involved in, be it

publishing, piano moving, or pea packing, has given me more insight into my fellow man than that of husbandry. Handling pigs, in particular, is a character-building experience, but housing, feeding, and penning the animals also contribute their share of mental gymnastics.

At one time or another I have received a hint, some advice, an anecdote, or some misinformation from just about everyone in town. This is understandable, because just about everyone in town has either raised pigs, or they have an opinion about the occupation (preoccupation). Most advice is well meant. Some of it you take, some of it you reject, and some of it you hang on a wall peg to marvel at when you have nothing better to do.

For example, the illustrations in the government pamphlet, *Raising a Few Hogs*, made pig raising look like a cinch. I still remember the hog trough that the pamphlet said "you can make from scrap lumber." In the line drawing it was a simple affair made by butt-nailing 2 two-by-eights together to form a V trough, and then nailing 2 more two-by-eights onto the ends to improve stability.

"Provide at least one-and-one-half feet of trough for each hog that you intend to raise," wrote the bureaucrat whose advice we were following. Evidently the man had never taken the time to observe pigs' table manners. The first thing we found was that the dominant pig at the trough will always attempt to hog the food by sprawling full length in the trough. Experience has shown us that spacer bars nailed in crosswise help. The dominant pig will still stretch his or her length on the trough, but the spacer bars keep his or her belly out of the food, and it provides rooter room for the other pigs to dislodge the ill-mannered one. Everyone needs rooter room. Like trough spacers, laws, customs, and common, ordinary manners serve to give us humans similar alternatives to assure that we use each other well.

Parsee Parson's advice is an example of the kind that you hang on a peg. He marches to the beat of a different drummer. Stopping by one day just as I finished feeding the pigs, he stood watching and then made one of his patented, one-of-a-kind observations.

"See how those pigs are all pushin' to the right?" he asked.

I watched as the six pigs at the trough leaned to their right until the farthermost one was popped off the end of the trough like an orange pip. The ousted one would immediately rush to the gap on the left and join his sibs in pushing the next one off. It seemed terribly egalitarian to me.

"Yeah, so?" I asked.

"That's a clear case of left-brained dominance!"

There was so little there that it only took a nanosecond for my brain to examine all the information it possessed on lateral brain dominance. "So what?" I asked somewhat testily.

"So nothin', I guess," he replied diffidently. "I noticed that same tendency when I had pigs, and I never did figure out how to build a right-handed trough."

I started to laugh but stopped when I saw that he was earnest. That was the thing about Parsee, he was always earnest, even when he was trying to build a right-handed pig trough. You have to know a little more about Parsee to know how to react to some of his ideas.

I remembered that I had been here about a year when I picked Parsee up as he was hitchhiking up from town. We had never talked before, but I knew that his place was on my way home. It was a brumal day, and for the first couple of miles we traveled in silence, just enjoying the sound of the truck's heater. Parsee waited until we were approaching his mailbox to say anything.

"Understand you're a writer?"

"Yeah," I answered reluctantly. At the time, I fostered an unspoken and, as it turned out, groundless fear that my writing would put local folks off.

"Good! I've got a job for you," he said as we pulled up to his driveway. "Want to come in for a cup of coffee?"

Incredulous, but ridden by the demon of an insatiable curiosity, I said, "Sure, why not?"

I had often passed Parsee's place and had noted that the exterior, with its neatly ordered garden, always appeared well kept. Inside, the house proved smaller than it looked from the outside, but the same sense of tidiness prevailed — except for one room. It was to that room that Parsee led me.

"Pardon the mess," he said as he took a pile of newspapers off a chair and put them on a nearby, ratty-looking file cabinet. "Have a seat while I make the coffee."

Distantly I could hear the sounds of coffee making as I seriously began to take in my circumstances. What I had taken for newspapers turned out to be copies of *The New York Review of Books,* and the presence of that sophisticated literary journal caused my eyebrows to lift. They lifted even farther as I let my eyes continue to pry into the man's reading matter.

What amazed me so was that there were only thirty-six books in the room, all with the same red cover, all housed compactly in a veneered bookshelf. They were a complete set of the *Encyclopedia Britannica,* 1948 edition. The clutter in the room was provided by knee-high stacks of the ubiquitous *New York Review of Books,* and a little more snooping revealed that Parsee was the subscriber addressee of the publication. It was speculation, but it appeared to me that he had every edition put out by that scholarly monthly.

Aside from an old photograph of a pleasant-looking

woman, whom I took to be Parsee's long-dead wife, there was nothing in the room but overstuffed furniture, the ratty file cabinet, and one of those abominable wood stoves whose functional square lines shout that the maker is afraid of being labeled old-fashioned. Most bachelors are spartan in their tastes, and this room was consistent. The reading material was not.

"Like it?" asked Parsee cheerfully as he came into the room bearing two mugs with steam streaming behind.

I wasn't sure whether he was referring to the decor or to the bizarre library, so I was noncommittal as I said, "You appear to have a serious interest in literary affairs."

"Oh, you mean these." He kicked at a pile of the *Review.*

"Well, yes. It appears that you've got almost every copy they published."

"Sugar or milk?" he asked as he put my mug down on a nearby stack.

"No, thanks."

He settled back into an overstuffed chair that molded to his slight frame, saying, "As far as I know I've got every one of'm, but I don't actually read'm. These . . ." he caressed the case of encyclopedias ". . . are my reading material during the winters. I'm on my third time through'm," he concluded matter of factly.

I must have goggled, for he hastened to continue rhetorically, "Where else would you look for the world's condensed knowledge than in the encyclopedia." He grinned triumphantly. "I take the *Review* for the personals — that's the job I have for you."

I strangled on the hot coffee. "What? . . . Why? . . ." I sputtered.

"You do write for a living, don't you?"

"Yes, but —"

He steamrollered on. "What I need is a couple of letters written," he explained earnestly. "I'm afraid I've gotten into a terrible rut with mine."

"Are you talking about me writing letters for you in
answer to the personals from the back of *The New York
Review of Books?*" I asked disbelievingly.

"Of course," he said. He rose and crossed to the ratty
file cabinet. "If you look at some of these, maybe you can
give me some . . . er . . . new slants." He opened the top
drawer.

"But, I —" The look he gave me was so naive and
earnest I shut up and was, against my saner judgement,
drawn to his side to look over his shoulder. The drawer
was filled with manila files whose tabs bore code numbers
that I recognized as footing each of the personal ads in the
Review.

"Look, Parsee, I —"

"Just have a look at some of them," he said cramming
a handful of files into my reluctant hands.

With a sigh, I gave in and shuffled through them as
I scrabbled in my mind for a way out of the dilemma. The
contents of the files nearly broke my heart. Each held a
single letter addressed in a hesitant longhand to an
anonymous female advertiser, and although the texts were
different, they all bore the same message. They were replete
with the usual adjectival clichés, "sincere," "secure," "seeking," and they all concluded with the inevitable, im-
ponderable, philosophical questions that began, "Do you
believe in . . . ?" In short, they were the maunderings of
a desperately lonely man.

Like the first taste of a cold glass of hard cider, the
deeper implications of what I was looking at struck me.
Suspecting, but fearful of what I would find, I opened the
lower drawer of the file cabinet and leafed through the

crammed contents of seventeen years of correspondence. The files were the same as those in the drawer above, and each held one or two pages of what appeared to be uncreased original correspondence.

"Where do you file the answers to your letters?" I asked hesitantly.

Parsee looked shocked. "Answers? Why, I would never mail these letters!"

"I see," I said, and I think that I honestly did.

That was several years ago, and the intervening winters have sharpened my skills at writing harmless letters to the lonely hearts in the personals. I've gotten pretty good at it, but I would just as soon never learn how good. Parsee hasn't changed. He continues to immerse himself in a protective womb of facts while constructing immutable questions (and unmailed letters) to which there are no risks of answers.

8

RISK IS A PIG ABANDONING one trough's contents (it doesn't matter to the pig whether it is a right- or left-handed one) for better pickings in another. This is one of life's lessons I acquired when designing "the world's sure-fire pig feeding system." It was well along in our fourth year of raising pigs when I discovered what, at the time, I thought to be *the answer*. It was simple. In order that each pig get its fair share, I spread the food out into two troughs.

But, as is the case with most sure-fire answers, it proved irrelevant. At the end of that growing season the pigs grew no faster, and if anything, I had used more feed. In a midwinter analysis of the problem, I concluded that having two troughs from which to choose (and run between) resulted in so much anxiety and frustration (not to mention exercise) that the pigs fretted off any weight gains they might have gotten from the system.

So, the following summer I undertook another, more commercial approach. Taking a lesson from the "demand" hog feeders that are available on the market, I rooted around my scrap metal pile until I uncovered an old, rusted-out lime spreader. From it I fashioned a commercial-type feeder with individual bins for eight pigs. Each bin, fed from the spreader body, had its own gravity-controlled lid that the pig had to lift with its snout. When the pig had taken as much as he wanted, he withdrew, and the lid would drop into a closed position. Besides saving a lot of feed hauling, this setup had the combined advantages of being weather- and rodent-proof. I carefully built in metal dividers between the bins that would prevent one pig from encroaching on his neighbor's bin.

After all this careful planning, I sported high hopes as I hooked it behind the tractor in the spring and dragged it out onto the field where we were going to pasture the pigs. Everything went like clockwork that day. We loaded the new feeder, brought the pigs to the pasture, and ac-tivated the electric fencing. It wasn't long before they discovered the food, and it took even less time for them to find out how to operate the lids.

I was understandably elated that evening when I went to bed, but that was the night I learned demand feeders encourage night feeding. All night long the lids banged in the pasture. I would just begin to drift off when, *slam! slam!* . . . *slamslam!* It soon got to the point where I stayed awake anticipating the next round of lid slamming, and by morning I was a red-eyed wreck.

Although he lives a good piece down the road from us, our neighbor, Harry Whatcher, stopped by in the fore-noon to ask if we had heard any poachers shooting deer during the night. When I pointed to the contraption in the field that had caused the ruckus, he contributed some rubber silencing strips and even helped nail them in place. He did not stay long enough to watch the pigs gnaw them off. Nor was he there when I threw in the symbolic towel, dragged the new demand feeder out of the field for further work on the drawing board, and replaced it with the quieter, two-trough system.

Now we haul feed, but we have settled for the mixed blessings of a demand waterer. This device has a valve that is activated by the pig's snout pressing on an attached paddle that is cradled in the bottom of the metal water bowl. Since pigs drink about three pounds of water for every pound of dry food consumed (lactating sows can use as much as ten gallons per day), the twice-daily chore of hauling water is a welcome omission.

As with the feeder, the pigs and I had to learn how to use the waterer. They learned faster than I did. Within an hour after I had run a plastic pipe out to a post where I had mounted the waterer, they had discovered the principle behind the source of supply. Instead of pressing on the waterer's paddle, they chewed the plastic pipe into something resembling the seven fountains of Rome and gamboled about in the resulting sprays.

I was onto them before they emptied our well that time. I elevated the new line out of their reach and delivered myself of a stern lecture. But I was not so lucky the next time. Having learned how the paddle worked, they showed some communal cooperation that belies the old saw that piggishness equals selfishness. It was a hot midsummer day when I went to take a shower and discovered that we had virtually no water pressure. I made a ranting, towel-draped exit from the house to discover that the pigs were taking turns standing on the paddle while their sibs lounged under the resulting overflow from the bowl.

The cost of replacing the water pump that burned itself

out when it had no water to pump has not stopped me from admiring our pigs' dedication to problem solving. My conclusions regarding this incident are shared by pigs the planet over. If the human race were to give an equal amount of energy and ingenuity to problem solving *our* basic needs, there would be no fear or famine in the world, even without pork on the menu.

9

THE SLEEPING BOAR'S SNOUT protruded below the lowest rail of the fence, and as I bent over to pick up my grain scoop I noticed a black ant purposefully legging it along the concrete less than an inch away from the ridge of cartilage that rimmed the boar's nose. Fascinated, I watched this intrepid ant pause at the foot of the climb, feel for handholds, and then do a classic bridging move up the chimney made by the boar's V-shaped lower lip . . . earthqua . . . qua . . . qua . . . ke! The boar twitched.

The ant paused to reconsider his route. Disaster yawned on his left, and to make the climb more perilous, a gale mounted as the boar began to snore. Girding up his abdomen, the ant did a layback ascent of the overhanging cartilage, and thereby narrowly avoided the avalanche of tongue that swept the boar's lower lip.

His antennae drooped with fatigue as he did a press-up to the level of the twin caverns in the face of the boar's nose. Spelunking is an ant's metier, and the little black devil perked right up when he saw the caves. Without a second thought for acclimatization, he legged his way right into the boar's left nostril, and he disappeared.

By this time I was down on my hands and knees to better witness this odyssey, and I barely heard the car pull into the dooryard. It was probably Burger McIntosh, the local vet, I speculated as I continued to stare at the point where the ant had disappeared. I had called the dour Scot vet earlier to make a house call to care for a scratch that had gotten infected on this same boar. He had been here before, I grumped as I kept my vigil. From his past visits, I figured that he would know his way to the holding pens here behind the barn.

"Mr. Schwenke . . . hello! . . . anyone home?"

"Damn!" I muttered. The stranger's voice was a woman's. "Back here," I yelled. I got to my feet brushing ineffectually at my dirty jeans and smelly frock, but I did not take my eyes from the boar's left nostril. There was still no sign of the spelunking ant.

The nubile young girl in the tailored white blouse, gray pleated midiskirt, and spectator pumps who appeared around the corner of the barn was the last thing I expected. In her wake strode a towering blond Adonis, resplendent in a sky-blue, three-piece leisure suit and an immaculate red tie. They were, I decided humbly, Grecian god and goddess who had gotten lost on their descent from Mount Olympus. Distracted, I nearly forgot about the ant.

"Ah," breathed the young girl, "Mr. Schwenke?" She thrust out a delicate, pink-tipped hand that smelled of Ivory soap.

My grunted assent sounded boarish and surly in my ears, and at the last second I remembered to take off my ratty old chore gloves before I took the soft hand.

"I'm Sherry, and this . . ." a brush of her hand wafted another zephyr of Ivory as she indicated her silent Olympian companion, "is Richard." She paused to take a deep breath that threatened the tailoring of the blouse. "We're from the Church of Latter Day Saints . . ."

"Of course," I muttered churlishly. I was chastising myself for not recognizing the Mormon missionaries' formula for proselytizing success: be neat; wear immaculate ties; and put the "looker" up front.

"I beg your pardon?"

"Nothing personal, Miss . . . Sherry. But, if you'll —"

"Our records indicate," she went on with a breathless rush, "that you are a member of the Church."

"Why, that was more than thirty years ago!" I snapped. Then my attention was claimed by the boar's left nostril as I thought I saw the antennae of the spelunker.

"That's why we are here," said the blond giant in a ringing tenor that would have made Bjoerling nervous. "We thought that if you prayed with us . . ."

The ant emerged onto a quivering nasal ledge, did a fast traverse, and using one antenna as an ice axe, began the climb of the remaining sheer face of the pig's nose. To the utter astonishment of the two missionaries, I dropped to my knees. In retrospect, I can imagine their exchange of looks as they joined me on the dewy ground.

"Dear God, we ask that You —"

I waved him to silence as I watched the ant cross the ledge of the snout and trek northward under the lower railing. I rose to keep better track of his progress up the pig's nose, and the Mormons rose with me. He took a class five-ten move over reverse exposure to cross the cornice of the boar's eyelid, and it was as though the ant knew that the climb offered no more comparable challenges. Atop the twitching boar's eyelid he paused to raise its antennae in the traditional victory clasp over his bald black head.

The ceremony over with, he shussed down the snowy white cheek of the boar and slalomed through the bristles back to the precipitous, terminal pitch of the nose. I went back down on my knees to see how he would manage the reverse of his laborous upward climb.

Behind me, the Mormon missionaries were indecisive, and I spared them a quick glance. I caught the significant patronizing look on the face of the young, nubile girl and the blond giant's perfectly raised eyebrow. The knees of the blond's sky-blue, three-piece leisure suit would require a cleaner's attention, I reckoned with some satisfaction.

"Look, Mr. Schwenke. If it would be better for you we could come b—"

Again I waved them off impatiently as I rivetted my attention on the ant. I heard them sigh resignedly, and in my peripheral vision I saw the blond looking for a drier place to kneel. The ant took an easier route down the sheer face and arrived at the nostril ledge in good shape. Then, as is always the way with climbers on the way down, he got cocky. Some attribute it to the euphoria, others say it is merely the altitude causing oxygen starvation of the brain. Whatever the reason, the ant was standing right in front of the boar's left nostril with his antennae again raised in the clasp of victory when the boar awoke with a tremendous sneeze.

Though it all happened in a split second, I followed the disaster right to its horrible conclusion. The ant, blown abdomen over thorax, bounced across the intervening ground and came to a brain-rattling arrest directly under the descending knee of the blond missionary.

"Look out!" I shouted too late.

He never knew what hit him.

The same could be said of the blond missionary and his young, nubile confederate when I threw them off the farm.

10

"IN A PIG'S EYE!" snorted Harry Whatcher. His hackles rose at my intimation that the Republicans couldn't carry Vermont in the upcoming Presidential elections. The phrase stuck in my head, but its etiology was of less importance to me at the time than pushing Harry's buttons. It was not until later that day when I was out in the field working on the pigs' electric fence that the phrase returned to plague me. An uncomfortable feeling at the back of my neck caused me to look over my shoulder.

One of the six pigs stood less than five feet behind me, and he had a look in his eye that I shall never forget. I have noted how uncannily human a pig's eyes are, but on this particular occasion I was obsessed with a plangent déjà vu. There was in that pig's eye a kind of empathic understanding that I had encountered only twice before in my life, and until now, only with humans.

The first time I met that look was as a young man in the occupation forces in Japan when in Kyoto I met a Zen Master. At the time I did not know much about Buddhists, and curiosity had taken me on a two-day liberty from Yokosuka, westward to the historic city, and thence, purely by happenstance, to the walled enclosure surrounding a Rinzai Zen temple. A thick door in the wall popped open, and a small, bearded man in a neat, brown kimono stepped out — right into my path. As I picked him up from the dust our eyes met, and there it was.

It happened in a split second. Without a word being spoken, there was an exchange of information, a sharing of our common lot, a sympathetic awareness. He smiled, touched me on the arm, and continued on his way. His touch left a warm tingle in my arm that stayed long after he disappeared from sight. At the time I did not know that he was a holy man, and it was only when I used my broken Japanese to describe his dress to a nearby rickshaw driver, that I learned that he was a Master. For me he remains nameless. I cannot remember what his features looked like; all I can remember are his eyes and the tingle.

Eight years later I met Hubert Dukes. Like the Zen Master, Hubert was a holy man — a Congregationalist minister from Berkeley, California. I entered Hubert's oak-lined study with a chip on my shoulder. I had just come from aggravating interviews with two other God Shop managers who had refused to preside over my nuptials because I had been divorced. It was hot, I had had my fill of mealy-mouthed pieties, and I was in no mood for further religiosity.

The moment I met Hubert Dukes' mild eyes, my irritation dropped away, I forgot my discomfort, and I knew Hubert was a friend. Polite, introductory conversation would have been superfluous at that point. We shook hands, and there was that same tingle. To make a long story short, Hubert married us and became a lifelong friend. Yes, I did once venture to tell Hubert about my experience with our first eye contact. His mild eyes crinkled up, and he smiled. He didn't say anything, he just smiled.

And now there was this pig. Unblinking, the faded blue eyes looked into mine, and I knew the same compassion, understanding, and love that I had experienced only twice before. I was afraid to move for fear of breaking the spell, and I continued to squat, looking back over my shoulder.

The pig's patience proved greater than my own. The hot August sun, my petrified joints, and my rational mind that had, until this moment, refused to pander to anthropomorphisms made me break the silence. "Good afternoon," I croaked with a dry throat. Nothing. The pig's knowing eyes never left mine.

It is not unusual or silly for a farmer to talk to his animals. What is unusual and silly is for the farmer to expect his animals to answer back, in English. "Hot, ain't it?" I ventured. Nothing — not so much as a blink. Sweat ran down the anxious crease lines between my eyes and dripped off my nose. It's the sun, I told myself. I've had too much, and I'm imagining things. But the pig's steady, unwavering eyes were not to be denied.

A car went by on the road. What would the driver see, I asked myself. He would see a farmer squatting down in the middle of an open field talking to, not with, one of his pigs — nothing remarkable. I shook off these extraneous thoughts and tried to recall details of the other two times this had happened to me. English ... maybe that, I reasoned, was the problem. I sorted back through thirty-four years of living to dredge up some rusty Japanese. "*Wakari ... ma ... sen?*" I asked hesitantly.

The eyes blinked.

Encouraged, I blurted out the only other phrases I could remember of the language. The first was the standard Japanese telephone greeting, and the last asked directions to the bathroom. Was there something to the Buddhist belief in reincarnation, I wondered?

The pig's eyes seemed to glaze.

Then I remembered the tingle. I had gone this far . . . why not? Ever so slowly I straightened up and approached the pig. The eyes never left mine. I knew that I was imagining things, but as I got closer I could have sworn that the eyes were developing a distinct Mongolian fold. I reached out and touched the coarse, wiry hairs between the understanding eyes.

He snorted his alarm. His snout came up with a snap, and I saved my fingers only by jerking my hand back at the last split second. I cursed the pig and my cupidity. He stayed only a second longer, but in that instant I saw only anger and fear in the pig's eye. Gone was the love and the charity and the Mongolian fold. But the tingle in my fingertips remained for the rest of the day.

11

I SAW LOVE AND CHARITY in my pig's eye; Freddy McIndoe, a firm believer, church deacon, and the brother of Mabel, saw Jehovah's righteous retribution in his. The four of us, Harry, Freddy, Noah, and I were hunkered in the milk parlor over to Whatcher's place when Freddy told us the story of his stolen sow with the two different-colored eyes. "Oneof'm," Freddy whined, "was blue, and tuther was gray. Warn't 'nother pig like 'er anywhere herebouts. That's why I named 'er Shermanlee . . . fer the Civil War gen'ruls," explained Freddy with a condescending look.

"Seems to me I remember the MacDonald sisters over to Jefferson Hill had a pig with different-colored eyes," observed Harry, pointedly pricking Freddy's story. As the largest landowner in town, Freddy's uppity ways, not to mention his screechy voice, went against the grain.

"MacDonald? . . . They related to Parsee Parsons?"

PIG OUT

Voracious guest wears welcome thin

By WILLIAM THOMAS

The Memphis Animal Shelter is fed up with its star boarder.

He weighs 350 pounds and he's getting fatter by the day.

He's got the biggest mouth on the place, and

By Dave Darnell

The inconvenient fella

not only does he eat enough to feed a horse, he also muscles in on the horse's plate.

He's on a diet of chicken noodle soup, dog food, pony chow and sweet mash. It is mixed in a glop and he eats it like a casserole-in-the-bucket.

The soup is donated by animal lovers. Yet, since September, he's run up a board-and-room bill of more than $450.

He's a hog.

He has eaten so much and stayed so long that his owner, who learned too late where he was, refuses to pay the bill to get him out.

The shelter is preparing to sell him, but Ron Cleaves, a supervisor, says it is doubtful that the city will break even. "We'll just accept the best bid, whatever it is, and let it go at that."

Cleaves leaves the impression that the shelter will make money just by getting rid of its biggest eater, which police found running loose on Warford Avenue on Sept. 9.

Although the Animal Shelter deals mostly in dogs and cats, it occasionally gets bigger, hungrier fauna. It now has five goats and a Shetland pony in addition to the boar hog. All will be sold to the highest bidders at noon, Dec. 9.

The animals live in a pasture behind the Animal Shelter at 3456 Tchulahoma. Cleaves said a spot is kept wet so the hog can play in the mud.

The pony has attracted the most interest. Bidders bring their children out to meet the pony, which has lived here for six months.

The pony is brown, has a blond mane and is the kind of animal that excites children this time of year.

The hog is something else.

"He's not pretty and pink," Cleaves admitted. "He's black and bristly."

And hungry.

**** The Commercial Appeal, Memphis, Wednesday, December 4, 1985

asked Noah, with a sly wink to Harry and me.

"Yup. First cousins," said Harry. "Parsee's arnt —"

" 'Arnt?' " I asked.

Harry stared at me like I'd lost my marbles. "Suah, arnt. His uncle was Harvey MacDonald, and . . ."

"Oh, you mean 'Aunt'," I said.

"That's what I said — arnt!"

I heaved a long-suffering sigh. I was tired of having my persistent downcountry pronunciation corrected, and I didn't think I could take another local genealogy session that seems to come up whenever Vermonters get together. "What happened to this pig of yours with the two differently colored eyes?" I asked Freddy by way of changing the subject.

"Murdered!" screeched Freddy abruptly.

Except for the inhale, exhale pump sounds of disinfectant rushing through the ranked teat cups in the sink, the milkhouse was suddenly still.

"Y'mean boochered, doncha Freddy?" asked Noah mildly.

"I mean Shermanlee was killed . . . shot . . . right in her own pen!" Seeing that he had finally claimed the group's attention, Freddy's eyes took on the fervor of a Groton preacher in the ecstatic throes of hellfire and brimstone, and his high-pitched whine dropped to a narrative plaint. "Parsee Parsons called me 'bout a month ago. Ast if I was missin' a pig . . . said he had one hangin' in that old barn've his . . . y'know the one I mean . . . that'n down from my place that he don't use n'more. Wal mistuh! I went down t'look, and there hung Shermanlee! . . . Deader'n a mackerel! . . . Bullethole right b'tween her differnt-colored eyes, and her right ham was gone!"

Whoosh . . . syyrrrrpwhoosh . . . syyrrp . . . . In the silence of the milkhouse the pulsating teat cup cleaner sounded loud.

Harry Whatcher's snort broke the silence. "You been suckin' at that cider ice again Freddy?"

It was a telling dig. Freddy's whispy eyebrows flapped like a moth at the porch light. Everyone knew of Freddy's incredible parsimony, and the story had long gone the rounds of the time when Freddy used to work at Seth Thomas's general store as clerk and general handyman. Seth made apple cider in the fall and would periodically subject it to freezing temperatures to hasten the "concentration of goodness," as Seth used to put it. Freddy's job was to remove the ice, ice that almost everyone knew was 90 percent water. As the story has it, Freddy would sneak the ice back to the place he shared with Mabel, thaw it, and they would serve it as cider to the rare guest that came along.

"Whoinhell," continued Harry, "would go to all the trouble of shootin' your ugly pig, haulin' it all the way down to Parsee's barn, string it up, and then only take one ham?"

Freddy teetered between indignation and righteousness. He settled for righteousness. "I ast m'self the same question at the time," he squeaked. "Fust thing off I thought've those hippies that moved onto the old Witherspoon homestead."

"Witherspoon?" said Noah ruminatively. "Related to the Witherspoons over to Goose Green?"

Whoosh . . . syyrrrrpwhoosh went the pump.

"The Withersp—" began Harry.

Freddy was not about to be denied his righteousness. He rode over Harry's genealogical riposte like Ethan Allen over Ticonderoga, "But then I knew it warn't the hippies, 'cause they was downcountry over the weekend. That only left—" The moths fluttered a dying gasp.

"You don't mean—" interrupted Harry, at last caught

up in the intrigue.

"Who else?" piped Freddy righteously.

"He wouldn't try somethin' like that — would he?" contributed Noah.

"Who're you talking about?" I sputtered in exasperation.

As a body they ignored me. Freddy continued, "Warn't no mistake. I sent Mabel over to borrer a cup a sugah, an' she saw the blood in the back've his pickup."

I shut up. I could see that no matter what I said they were going to continue to refer to the "murderer" in the third person. Third-person references are a maddening habit of rural folks who have lived through the era of the telephone party line. Gossipping, an honorable preoccupation in the country, became hazardous when the gossipers found that using names on the communal line got them in hot water. In self-defence they developed and refined third person references to a fine point. Today the state-of-the-art is to see how obtuse one's references can be to another person and still communicate the meaty stuff.

"Wait a minute," interrupted Noah. "If we're talking about the same feller, he died last week."

"That's right!" chortled Freddy. "Nuts busted off'n the downside rear wheel've his John Deere when he was balin' that steep bank up behind his upper field."

"Jeezumcrow!" breathed Harry with a shiver. As a farmer he knew the hazards of steep ground and heavy farm machinery. "Did it flip?"

"Twice!" Freddy was positively ecstatic.

Noah's long, seamed face reflected his distaste. "You'd've made a demned good undertaker, Freddy," he growled.

Oblivious to the tangible tension in the room, Freddy's high falsetto continued, "That Deerey ended up on his chest, and Doc Macpherson says that it must've taken a couple've hours for him to die." He paused long enough to draw a huge, drawn-out sigh. "When I heard about it, I could see Shermanlee's two different-colored eyes starin' at me, and I knew that that God does work in mysterious ways."

Harry's mouth screwed up as though he had just swallowed a tablespoonful of horseradish. When he finally spoke, his voice grated with his effort at heartiness. "Y'seen my new Miss Dairy Queen poster I glued up outside the milkhouse?"

Noah's horsey face took on a funny look — one that must have matched my own.

"Why, no," said Freddy.

It was satisfying to see how fast Freddy's righteous indignation gave way to lust.

"Let's have a look-see." Freddy rose and stepped out of the door.

"Faugh!" said Harry as he slammed the door and tripped the lock on the inside.

"Yup," said Noah with a sickly smile, "God does work in mysterious ways."

12

NOAH SLACK AND AARON SLACK are as different as a
kernel of Country Gentleman corn and the corn on your
little toe. Noah prizes the old ways; Aaron, his son, the
new. Noah will spend hours carving an axe helve from a
piece of ash to save the price of store-boughten one. Aaron
will spend the same amount of time shopping around for
the best bargain in a new pickup, which he can't afford
in the first place.

Though he lived in a run-down trailer on a half acre
of the old homestead, a piece of land begrudgingly donated
by Noah, Aaron has never owned a pickup that was more
than two years old. The chromework always gleams, and
the gun rack always sports a new 30-30 come hunting
season. Aaron is proud of his trucks.

Some folks say he is too proud. Talk has it that his
three kids go without winter clothes so that Aaron can perk

up his latest pickup with those flashy running lights, or
so that he can purchase a set of those new, wide, fat tires
with the racing lugs on the chrome rims. They also say
Aaron has a drink or two too many.

But small town folks are sometimes small-minded, and
they exaggerate. Aaron came out of high school with so-
so grades, with an ambition as big as the size thirteen
sneakers he wore on the basketball team, and with Darlene
Tameleo, whom he had gotten pregnant three months
before the senior prom.

From that point on things went sour for Aaron. He
married Darlene and took a seasonal job with the town
road crew. Come fall he got done with the road crew and
faced the long winter without a job. He managed to get
through by finding piecework cutting cordwood. In the
spring he went to help Noah tap his sugar bush and boil
off, and when that petered out with the trill of the spring
peepers, he hired on with Harry Whatcher to drive tractor for the corn planting.

But there never seemed to be enough money or jobs
to go around, and Darlene always seemed to be pregnant.
Sue had had Darlene and Aaron in her first kindergarten
fourteen years ago, and she noted ruefully that even back
then "Darlene had never been able to keep her pants on."

Like most of us, Aaron and Darlene kept an extensive
garden, chickens, and a pig or two. Last spring I arranged
with Vern The Pig Man to come over and pick from the
newest litters, and when I arrived, I met Aaron and Noah
coming up from the farrowing pens with a bran sack full
of squeal. Back in the direction from which they had come
I heard the sounds of Vern's trumpet.

"Aaron, aren't you afraid of getting that brand new
truck dirty?" I asked jokingly.

"Nope," replied Aaron cheerfully, "pigs is naturally

clean animals, and there ain't one that'd dare shat on a new Jimmy."

"And besides that," added Noah, "he's got newspapers spread from one end to tuther."

We exchanged a few more pleasantries and went our separate ways. I took the lidded apple crates I used for piglets down to the farrowing pens where Vern greeted me unenthusiastically. I always suspected that Vern sold his pigs only out of sheer necessity. Parting with them was almost too much for him. Since we had already settled on a price, there remained only, in Vern's words, "the pickin' and ketchin' ".

It was commonly acknowledged that Vern kept the cleanest pig operation in town. His farrowing pens were made up with old iron pipes, but he painted them regularly, and one seldom found more than a couple of hours worth of accumulated manure anywhere around.

The sow that threw the litter I was chosing from was eating contentedly in her pen. She had been moved over from the V-shaped farrowing enclosure where she had birthed and where she was lodged while the babies suckled. Cleverly arranged bars in the farrowing area kept her from lying down or rolling on the newly born pigs, and the gap between the floor and the bottom rung allowed the babies the run of the pen they were now in.

They were a sprightly lot of five-week-old youngsters. When I climbed into their pen they stopped their mauling play to stare at me, and I suddenly became aware of the overall silence. Looking around, I found that every pig in the place, big and little, had stopped what he or she was doing and was looking my way.

"Makes you want to check that your fly is buttoned, doesn't it?" I observed in an aside to Vern.

"Um," grunted Vern as he stroked his full black mustache with his trumpet.

I looked at my host and found his beady little eyes staring at me with the same intensity as the pigs. "Do you always carry that horn around?" I asked with a trace of unease.

"It settles them down after a ruckus," he replied. "Watch!" He nestled the mouthpiece up under his mustache, and his cheeks puffed into pink ping-pong balls as he launched into "Sweet Georgia Brown." He was ragging the line about four bars into the piece before I realized that every pig in the place had resumed what he was doing before I stepped into the pen. As the last sweet note drifted off, I sighed. I envied both Vern's musical skills and his unique empathy with pigs.

It seemed a shame to interrupt the tranquility of the place again, but I was anxious to get the pigs home and settled in their new home. The first piglet I chose was relatively easy to catch, but her shrill shrieks as I held her up by her two hind legs and passed her over to Vern for crating brought the house down. The sow was grunting frantically while trying to stand on her hind legs, and she was encouraged by a manic chorus from her brothers and sisters farther down the line of pens.

Under the pressure of the din I worked as rapidly as I could, but it is never easy, even in the best of times, to sort the piglet you want out from the frantic pile of squirming bodies. The skill required to catch a scurrying piglet by the hind leg is akin to snatching an arrow out of midair, and when the rooting section is on the other side, it increases the difficulty by a factor of two.

At last it was done, and to the soothing strains of "Sweet Georgia Brown," I lugged the noisy crates up the hill and slid them into the back of my old pickup. Vern joined me there for the ritualistic passing of the money, and in the ensuing conversation I made an amazing discovery about Vern The Pig Man: away from the pigs he was just like anyone else. He talked about the weather, exchanged a little gossip about the lechery of an errant school board member, and passed on a recipe to Sue for bread pudding.

He reverted to form as I got in and started the truck. "Take it easy on these back roads," he warned. "Those crates are hard, and piglet psyches bruise easily."

I laughed alone. "What about Aaron?" I asked with a defensive grin. "Transporting pigs in a bran sack isn't the most comfortable ride."

"Whuff," snorted Vern disgustedly. "When I saw that damned poke I charged him five dollars more per pig!"

I was still laughing as I pulled out of his dooryard, but I subconsciously kept my speed down as I traveled down Scotch Hollow Road. A mile from Vern's place the tarmac makes a dog-leg curve around Gideon Whitman's place, and I was going slow enough to see the crowd gathered there well in advance (five people — six, counting myself — make a crowd in the outback of Newbury). The center of attention was Aaron Slack's new truck and the wreckage of the west end of Gideon's old house. It appeared as though Aaron had tried to take his new GMC truck straight through the dog-leg, and had only gotten as far as Gideon's four-poster in the bedroom.

When I saw the state trooper's car I shut down and got out. I came around the hood of my truck just in time to avoid the piglet that shot between my legs, but I was unable to avoid Gideon's two grandkids. They were, as they explained later when they were helping me up out of the culvert, in hot pursuit. One made a dive for the escaped piglet and knocked my left pin out from under me, and while I was spinning like a top, the second caromed off the first and took out my right.

Fortunately we were at the end of mud month, the culvert was relatively dry, and I was wearing my go-get-pigs clothes. As I brushed myself off I took in the scene. The delighted cacophony of pig and kid squeals nearby contrasted starkly with the gloomy tableau across the road.

Aaron was leaning on the ruined remains of his new truck with a thunderous look on his face; Gideon was seated on a rusty anvil morosely contemplating what remained of his bedroom, and Noah was gesticulating at the state trooper while delivering himself of a monologue.

As I drew nearer I made out the disbelieving look on the young trooper's face and heard the suppressed laughter in Noah's voice as he was saying, ". . . the demned bag come loose, and thet little bugger got hisself wedged down there b'tween the brake and the gas pedal . . . accident pure and simple!"

The trooper tipped his Smoky Bear hat further down over his eyes as he scribbled in a notebook. I suspected that he was trying to hide the sceptical look in his eyes. "All right, Mr. Slack," he said finally. "Thank you for your statement." He looked around the group and put away his pencil. "I guess that about wraps it up. I have all your statements, and the wrecker will be along in a few minutes."

He shrugged his leather belt around where he wouldn't be sitting on his gun and got into his car. "I don't think the boy's been drinking," he added through the open window, "and that cockamamie story is just far-fetched enough to be true." He reached for the ignition, and over the roar of the starting engine, I heard him mutter, "But I'd love to be a fly on the wall when he tries to explain it to his insurance agent."

Together we sorted things out. I took Noah and Aaron's piglets over to Aaron's, and on the way home I recalled Vern The Pig Man's parting shot. Indeed it didn't pay to buy a pig in a poke.

13

WHEN I FIRST SUMMED IT UP, I thought that the accident resulted in nothing but pluses. Aaron's insurance got him another new truck to fret over, and it covered the cost of the repair of Gideon's house. Gideon had to move out while young Tom Roberts, the hippie living over on Jefferson Hill, did the fixing, but it was spring, and it didn't seem likely that the plumbing would freeze up while Gideon was gone. As for young Tom, he needed the work. God knows he needed the work.

While Tom worked, Gideon moved in with his kids, Perley and Joy Whitman. The trailer had gotten too small, and Perley had moved his family into a tenement in the village. I figured that nothing could have been better for Gideon than being around those two hot-pursuiter grandchildren, but I hadn't given enough thought to Perley. The word around town was that Perley wasn't overly pleased

with the arrangement but acquiesced because there wasn't
anywhere else for the old man to go.

In view of what has happened since, I think that it was
Perley's rumored reluctance that frosts me most. I know
that Perley is on hard times, that he lost his job at the mill
when he cut his leg with a chainsaw, and that he has two
kids to support, kids on whom he dotes. But parental devotion should work both ways. Too often hereabouts it
doesn't.

It's ironic that it was Gideon who started me thinking about one-way parental devotion. At a town school
meeting a few years back I opposed what I thought was
an extravagant increase in the school budget, and during
a recess from the proceedings, Gideon buttonholed me and
read me the riot act. "What you're proposing is penny-
wise and pound-foolish," he pontificated. "What would
we be without our kids?" he asked rhetorically.

At the time I kept my existential thoughts to myself,
and I'm glad I did. Gideon was speaking honestly from
personal experience. He set great store by Perley, his first
kid, who was then in the senior class at the high school.
Maybe it was because I lost the ensuing vote by a considerable margin, but Gideon cooled off quickly, and when
the meeting was over he came over to mend fences. "I hear
that you're aimin' to raise piglets — gonna take a sow and
boar through the winter?"

He was retired now, living off a meager Social Securi-
ty check, but in his time Gideon was the best swineherd
in the north country of Vermont. Even Vern The Pig Man
admitted that when he was up a stump he went to Gideon
for advice. So, though my proposed budget cut had lost
disastrously, I was pleased to have him broach the subject
of my new pig project. His counsel was to go ahead with
the scheme, but to keep a close eye on the feed bill, and

he generously promised to come by in the spring when the sow farrowed.

Gideon's wife, Helen, died on the day that my sow gave birth to thirteen squirming babies. I know that only because I called minutes after the ambulance had come to take her body away. Embarrassed, I appologized for calling at such an awkward time, and he did his best to assure me that it was all right. "It's fittin'," he said, "for new life to come along to replace an old one that got done." Looking back on our painful conversation that day, I find it fitting that Gideon did not draw a distinction between pigs and people.

He often made pig analogies. I remember that when, after the funeral, he came over to see the new litter, the sadness in his eyes receded a little as he watched thirteen white little sausages cavort around in their bed of clean sawdust. "See that one," he pointed towards the most active of the bunch. "He's like Perley. He's the skater of the litter."

"Skater?"

"Yup. Didn't you never hear the one 'bout bein' as independent as a hog on ice?"

I laughed.

"That one," he predicted, "will be the first one off the tit and the first one to push mom off the feed trough when he gets enough heft."

Gideon couldn't have been more right or prophetic. Three weeks after the accident — just a week before Tom Roberts was to finish the repair work on the old place — I needed to know how to build a lightweight, portable graze fence for the young pigs. If anyone would know how to build it, it would be Gideon. I remembered that he was staying over to Perley's, but Perley's phone had been disconnected when he lost his job at the mill. The need for the information was urgent. At eight weeks, those baby pigs were developing an appetite that was going to put me in the poorhouse, so I hopped into the truck and drove over to Perley's.

Perley's dooryard was a mess. Old rusted cars, minus a hood here, a door there, littered the spaces between gigantic lilac bushes. Someone, somewhere back before the place had become a rental slum, had taken a great deal of pride in those lilacs, but now they were all gone to sucker growth. I parked between a discarded pickup bed and a huge pile of children's toys. As I got out I looked disbelievingly at the toys. It was an incredible collection of wheeled vehicles: bikes, trikes, cars, trucks, tractors. They had two things in common, each was plastic, and each appeared to be broken. It was a graveyard of toys. It was almost as though the kids were being prepared to emulate their elders.

On the granite doorstep Perley's two kids were fighting loudly over who would get the last crumbs from a bag of potato chips, but when I said hello, they abruptly turned coy and shy. The TV blared from beyond the screen door, and I knocked in vain.

The smallest of the duo grinned impishly at his brother and upended the potato chip bag on his head. Screaming with glee, they disappeared around the corner of the house, leaving the bag and remnants on my shoes. They were, to use Gideon's phrase, "real skaters."

"Oh, hi, Mr. Schwenke," came Joy's voice from the dark inside the house. "I dint know you was there . . . Perley! Perley! Mr. Schwenke's here!" she yelled.

"Hello, Joy. Don't bother Perley. I was just looking for Gideon."

Joy didn't answer, and I couldn't see inside, so I waited on the doorstep. Minutes passed, and finally Perley appeared on the other side of the screen. He wore a red undershirt, and although it was midday, he looked as though he had just gotten up. I couldn't see well enough through the screen mesh, but if what folks intimated was true, and I suspect it was, his eyeballs matched his shirt.

"What can I do for you, Mr. Schwenke?" he asked.

"I was looking for your dad," I replied. "I need some help with a pig problem."

Perley's blunt finger played with the frayed edge of a hole in the screen. "He don't live here no more," said Perley, his voice getting gravelly.

"Did he go back home?"

"He's in a home awright," snorted Perley. "He was gettin' see-nyle, so me'n Joy decided to send him down to the Haven Rest Home in Bradford."

My stomach knotted suddenly, and the bitter question on my lips went unasked as the kids reappeared shrieking, "Bang . . . bang . . . you're dead!"

"I'm not!"

"Y'are so!"

"Kids!" said Perley piously. "What would I be without my kids?"

14

SOMEHOW THE CYCLES need to be interrupted. New blood needs to be introduced. Pig breeders call it "breaking the in-and-in breeding cycle." If you repeatedly breed within the same or related stock, you are asking for trouble.

Tom and Mary Roberts are new blood for Newbury's tired old in-and-in cycles. Formerly a Philadelphia bank clerk and receptionist, respectively, Tom and Mary came here in the flush of the back-to-the-land movement. They arrived in the early seventies in a cloud of fuzzy thinking mixed with the fumes of their sick VW bus and the cloying sweet scent of pot.

"Those hippies who built the camp on the old Whatcher place over on Jefferson Hill," was the way that the local folks referred to them. Flower children had come and gone in Newbury, and even the most optimistic, myself included, said that they would go on their way within a year. But they stuck. It's been twelve years now, and although they are struggling, they are still trying to live out the dream they arrived with.

The local reaction has been a fascinating study in assimilation. Old-timers were the first to stop referring to their self-built house as a "camp" (in local parlance a camp is a temporary summer-occupancy structure). When Mary took a nearby waitressing job to supplement the income from Tom's erratic handyman-carpentry jobs, everyone agreed that they "showed a lot of courage." And Tom's prowess with a softball bat is prized by the ex-jocks and other townspeople who flock to the nightly summer softball games at Mills Memorial Field. The other day I even heard old "four generations" Harry Whatcher refer to their place as "the Roberts Place," a sure sign that they have arrived.

I heard my first shaggy-pig story from Tom Roberts, and it's worth repeating here to show to what lengths people will go when living out their dreams. I had stopped by to see how the piglets I had sold Tom were doing, and after we had looked over the progeny, Mary insisted that I stay for supper. "We're having pizza," she announced enthusiastically. There was no convenient out. Mary had once swapped me a loaf of homemade bread for a quick blacksmithing job that I did for Tom, and the memory of that piece of lead still haunted me.

My only hope, I rationalized as I accepted, was that her job waitressing in a pizza joint might have converted her to a leavened white flour crust. It hadn't, and the crust wasn't. At the end of the main course I chose the coward's course. "Delicious . . . tastes . . . er . . . healthily nutritious," I effused in a voice loud enough to drown out the borborygmous sounds from my indignant stomach. I eyed the heavy mugs of rose hip tea and the servings of maple tofu cheesecake warily.

Pig anecdotes are standard post-dinner fare in farm country, and Tom began to relate the story of purchasing his first pig at the livestock auction at East Thetford. His rubbery face mimed their surprise when they were told that they were expected to take the pig off the premises that same night.

My own face reflected his surprised expression as I said, "Why this isn't bad." I was staring at the tofu cheesecake.

Mary glowed.

"We've made a lot of mistakes in this homesteading venture," said Tom with a laugh. "I remember coming home with the pig — we drove all the way with the pig loose in the back seat — she crapped or peed at every mile marker on the interstate. Then, when we got here we realized that we didn't know what or how to feed her."

"And yet we had this romantic dream," added Mary. "I can't believe how naive we were. We scrimped and saved for almost three years in the city to put together a big enough nut to make the move to the country. We were going to buy a little piece of land, grow or raise all of our own food, and live off the fat of the land. That pig was our first move."

"Well, it seemed to make sense at the time," said Tom. "I had read all these homesteading books, and they all said that the family milk cow and a pig are the 'cornerstones of the successful homestead venture.' " He grimaced wryly. "One description that I remember particularly was a writer who called pigs 'mortgage lifters.' "

"Oh, oh," said Mary, "I can feel Tom's shaggy-pig story coming on."

I mashed up the remaining crumbs of the cheesecake between the tines of my fork and said, "I'm an appreciative audience if I'm properly fed. Got any more cheesecake?"

"Me too," said Tom. "And some milk to go with. Will you have some too?" he asked. "I'm sorry, but we don't have the cow anymore, and this commercial stuff is a poor substitute."

I declined.

"Well, it all started with that pig," began Tom as Mary went out to the kitchen to replenish our plates. "We had taken the first step, so that very night we decided to add a milk cow to our homestead. The following week we borrowed a trailer from Charlie Daniels and went back to the auction for a milker.

"We bought her on the basis of how cowy she looked," yelled Mary from the kitchen.

"Looking back, I can't believe how lucky we were. We were real babes in the woods. That little Jersey turned out a gallon and a half of milk at every milking."

"We were literally swimming in milk," laughed Mary in the distance.

"At first it was really nice, y'know. All the milk we could drink — and all that cream! But then it began to pile up. We made butter, cottage cheese, and cheese, and then fed the whey to the pig. But it kept coming. We made ice cream and milk shakes. In desperation I tried making house paint that used milk as a base. Eventually we got so we couldn't look at a glass of milk. It even got to the point that for a while the pig would turn up her nose at the slops if they were drowned in milk."

"But I've never seen a pig put on weight faster than that one did," said Mary as she put a huge slice of the cheesecake in front of me.

"It was plain to see that we needed help," continued Tom, "so we went back to the auction and bought another pig. That really balanced things out — for a while. Then the cow's production started to go down. Until then we had ignored the basic facts of why a cow produces milk. Our homestead reference books told us that we could reasonably expect our family cow to produce for about ten months out of the year, and then it had to be freshened with a new calf."

"Before we had really thought it through," said Mary taking up the tale, "we called the artificial inseminator people and had her impregnated. Then, as the time for the calving drew near, some of the implications began to sink in. One butcher pig requires relatively few capital expenditures, but a cow is something else. There's fencing, shelter, hay, breeding fees, and the big chunk of money you plunk down for the animal itself."

"You forgot the insurance on the structures and the prorated real estate taxes," I added around a mouthful of cheesecake.

"Three tons of hay and over a ton of grain! That's what it takes each year to feed a cow properly!" growled Tom indignantly.

"And that doesn't take into account the grazing space," pointed out Mary. "But we were into it, and I have to admit we really liked milk. We put our heads together and decided to follow the whole thing through to its logical conclusions."

"Which were?" I prompted.

Tom flushed. "We went back to the auction and bought another milker to cover the first milker's dry spell."

"So now you had a pregnant milker that was ready to deliver and a second one, not to mention the two pigs," I summed up.

"Six pigs," amended Tom with a grin. "At the auction we got to worrying about the flood of milk we would have when the two cows' production overlapped, and we bought four more."

"One of which was a boar," interrupted Mary.

"We got rid of him in midwinter when he got randy."

"But not before he had impregnated two of the sows."

Tom sighed heavily and made a face at the taste of the milk in his glass. "By midsummer of the following year we had two cows, a Hereford-Jersey calf that we intended to put down in the freezer a year later, four sows, and nineteen baby pigs."

"We learned a lot over the winter though," said Mary with a sardonic smile.

"Yeah, we nearly lost the calf to pneumonia. It was too late then, but we found out that the barn was too big to house that few animals at thirty-below temperatures. First thing next summer we put in a partition to cut down the space that the cumulative animal body heat would have to heat, but it was still too big, especially after we sold most of those baby pigs."

"We'd never have been able to afford all that haying equipment if we hadn't made some profit off those piglets," said Mary.

"That's the trouble with this shaggy-pig story," observed Tom ruefully. "When you take it all apart, each step makes sense, but altogether . . . ." He shrugged eloquently. "Take that haying equipment, for example. All winter long we'd been buying hay, and we were damn near broke when sugaring came around. I figure that we now get our hay at about one tenth of the cost we were putting out before. Homesteading really makes you sharpen your pencil."

"And wears out your eraser," I contributed from my own experience. "Didn't I hear that somewhere along the way you were in the business of custom-cutting hay?"

"Yup. That came about after we added three sheep and a goat."

"A goat!" I echoed.

"And a dozen chickens," put in Mary. "What's a homestead without chickens?'

Tom's eyes glazed over as he remembered. "You see what I mean? We got the sheep to fill out the thermal necessities of the barn, and when we realized we were short of hay land to feed everyone, I started cutting our neighbor's hay on shares. As for the goat, I had read that they did a job in reclaiming old, overgrown pasture land, and we have an acre that needed a strong forager to make it viable to grow hay."

"I begin to see what you mean by a shaggy pig story. You started out with a pig and ended up with a goat, three sheep, two milk cows, a calf, a dozen chickens, and God only knows how many pigs," I marveled.

"That was at the beginning of the following winter," laughed Tom. "It turned out that two of the ewes were pregnant, and each threw twins in the spring."

I sat back, stomach and brain sated to overflowing. "Phew!" I wheezed. "So what did you do then?"

"I went to work waiting table," said Mary, "to pay for the extra fencing that we needed for the sheep."

"Not to forget the extra waterers, feeders, buckets, hayforks, the costs of mechanical breakdowns, shearing equipment for the ewes . . . it was all just too much!" sighed Tom. He stared at his half-emptied milk glass with distaste.

"The saga came to a head one night when we were sitting around the table here looking at the unfinished walls of the house," Mary smiled. "We had inseminated the second milk cow with another Hereford cross because we wanted to be able to put down fresh beef every year, and we were calculating how many ewes could be serviced by a ram." Mary's eyes were unfocused on the middle distance. "I remember Tom lifting his head out of a reference book on sheep breeding and saying, 'a ram can service a dozen or more ewes'! Maybe it was the way he said it . . . y'know, kind of awed." Mary's eyes focused suddenly, and she colored. "Anyways, here we were bustin' our buns to let our livestock have kids, and the kid that we had talked about having ourselves wasn't even in the planning stage. We had gotten so involved in the livestock we didn't even have time to finish off the inside of our house."

I looked around me and saw that the varnish on the trimwork and the paint on the walls were all sparkling new. I felt Tom's eyes on me, and when I returned his look, I saw that there was a matching sparkle there.

"Yup. It's all newly done. We sold every bit of livestock on the place. And," he paused to hug his wife. "And now . . . Mary's pregnant."

I offered my congratulations but was unable to resist asking, "So how come you bought pigs from me this year?"

"Dreams die hard," said Mary with a sly look at Tom. "We decided to celebrate my pregnancy with just a couple of pigs around the place."

Tom was glaring at the half-empty milkglass in front of him. "I'd give a lot for a decent glass of milk!" he growled. "Maybe . . . what if . . . ?"

15

Handmaiden: "1. A personal servant . . . .
2. That which serves as an aid."

The American Heritage Dictionary

A LOT OF PEOPLE GO TO RAISING PIGS with less
knowledge about what they are doing than Tom and Mary.
I remember the vet, Burger McIntosh, telling me the story
about breeding the Burnsteins' first-ever pig. It was a funny
story, one that with hindsight, I suspect, was designed to
mitigate the bill that he later submitted for looking at a
persistent lameness in one of our pigs (mild arthritis).

Sal and April moved here in the mid-seventies, and they
pretty much keep to themselves. For young people, they
are remarkably reserved — one might even say stuffy —

and they take themselves very seriously. They bought a year-old sow from Burger, and, according to Burger, "they dinna know the frrront end a'the pig frrrom the rearrr." Burger's Scots burr was as thick as the heavy gray eyebrows that he used effectively to emphasize his inveterate storytelling.

"Coome Octoberrr they rrrang me oop, and the missus says they canna bearr to kill tha poor thing, did I ken anywa who had a booor that they could mate theirrr sow wi. I says, 'Aye. Yourrr neighbor, Vern, has a bonny booor.' 'How,' she asked, 'do we ken when she is rrready for sairvice?' "

I fixed Burger with a sceptical look. "April and Sal are city people. I can't imagine April asking when a sow is 'ready for service'."

"Aye," admitted Burger impatiently, "I believe her exact words werr . . . er . . . 'make love.' "

I stilled my laughter under his dour look.

"I descrribed the sow's rrredness and swelling arrroun' the vulva, grooonting, and general nairvousness when in heat," he continued sternly. " 'Peak fairtility,' I told her, 'coomes when the sow stands wi'out moving when you prrress doon on her back. When tha' happens, the sow must be sairviced immediately, and you should ta'the pig to Vern's booor.' "

I quaked with suppressed laughter. All pig growers know that vets recommend moving pigs as casually as marriage counselors recommend a divorce, and both are conspicuously absent come moving time. "How did you recommend they transport their sow over to Vern's?" I asked.

"By pickoop, a'course," he snapped. "Weel! Missus Burnstein rrrang me oop a couple of months later t'say that they had had a leetle trouble loading the animal, but that they had managed. Now, the missus said, they were

wurried that their sow hadna taken. I rrrecommended
rrrepeating the sairvice as often as necessary, and I suggested
that she handmate the pairrr t'be sartain."

My laughter bubbled over. The mental picture I had
of April Burnstein in Vern's servicing pen was more than
I could bear. With all that fat between themselves and their
working end, boars have notoriously bad aim, and handmating is a technique in which the swineherd manually
assists the boar in the insertion of his penis.

Burger kept a straight face, but his bushy eyebrows
were doing flip-flops as he said, "The lassie obviously dinna ken handmating, so I explained. She hung oop on me!"
He finally broke down and joined me in laughter.

"I met the mister downstreet a day or so later," he
added, "and he said they'd boochered the sow the following day."

16

LIFE-IS-EARNEST, LIFE-IS-REAL folks like April and Sal Burnstein should never raise pigs. It is an occupation that, in its traditional small-scale sense, is best left to hopelessly bent romantics. And that, I think, best defines the anachronistic small-scale farmer.

By contrast, the modern agribusinessman has no problems with manufacturing units of pork. He sits at his computer measuring out genes, food, and water and projects weight gain, market trends, and profits. There are no troubling moral life/death questions for this shadowy figure. Everything is hermetically encapsulated in an electronically ledgered spreadsheet. He too is of the life-is-earnest, life-is-real school, but he is protected from reality by buttons and remote pulses of electric current.

There is no such remoteness for the husbandryman. Until now, man has had to confront the moral dilemma

of the ritual killing. Man found that the rationalization of
the hunt disappeared when he started penning in animals
as a dependable meat source. Domestication had attendant
pitfalls. It bred familiarity, even love. And, because of the
ritual killing, it occasionally bred vegetarianism.

Vern The Pig Man is not a vegetarian. He loves his
pigs — literally to death. "How can you do it?" I asked
him one afternoon. "How can you get so attached to these
pigs and then slaughter them?"

Vern's answer was to pick up his horn and play "You
Always Hurt The One You Love." That old chestnut from
the Glen Miller era was only the first of many pig insights
that Vern would contribute over the years to my educa-
tion. He was being facetious, but it had a kernel of truth
in it. The corollary of love is hate, and, given the right
circumstances, pigs can generate a lot of the latter.

Moving pigs from one location to another is a case in
point. No other chore of the small-scale pig raiser evokes
more genuine hate than this one. Understandably, it also
stimulates the mystical side of the swineherd. Old almanacs
are a wonderful source for this folklore. One that I con-
sulted warned that pigs should not be moved when the
moon was full; another swore that swine could be easily
led if the dominant pig (there is a pecking order amongst
pigs) was crossed between its eyes with an ear of corn that
is in dent. I always figured that the ear-of-corn bit was
nothing more than Missus Page's applied psychology, "You
don't ketch a pig, you fetch it." Likewise for the one that
says that if you "tap a sweet apple on the snout of a swine,
it will follow." Trying the latter almost cost me a hand.

Being an incurable optimist, I cannot resist trying out
even the most far-fetched of these panaceas. Seth Thomas's
IGA store is a treasure house of such lore. Old-timers, mostly retired dairy farmers who quit when refrigerated bulk

tanks replaced separators and milk cans, divide their time between the bench on the porch of the IGA and one of the padded stools at the counter in the drugstore.

I got a lot of information on the porch of Thomas's IGA, some useful, some downright libelous. It was Seth himself who once told me that his father used to lead pigs with a four-foot piece of baling twine. He politely ignored my derisive snort, and went on to wait on another, less skeptical customer. Seth is clever. He makes his living from knowing his customers, and he had me pegged as a *peculiar one* with a penchant for pig lore.

I bought a box of corn flakes that I didn't need and returned to the register. "How'd he do it?" I asked as he rang up my purchase.

"Do what?" he countered guilefully.

"Lead a pig with a four-foot piece of baling twine." I kept my cool, determined not to buy another box of corn flakes.

"Oh, that." The tone of his voice dripped innocence, but his businessman's eyes were coldly sizing me up. Evidently he failed to find even a Baby Ruth in my eyes, for he said with a shrug, "I was just a kid. As I recall, he tied the twine to her leg."

"Her leg?" I parroted incredulously.

"And he would . . . sort of . . . tug on it when the pig was going the wrong way. You need some milk to go on those corn flakes?"

Without milk, either of the cow or human kindness sort, I went out to my truck snorting disbelief. At least, I told myself, I won't have to come back to Thomas's IGA for corn flakes for a while — if ever. But as I was driving home, I got to wondering if it might . . . nah! . . . but? . . . whatthehell! . . . never hurts to give something a try. What could I lose but four feet of baling twine?

That afternoon when I went out to feed the pigs, I carried with me a length of baling twine. As always, crossing the electric fence that surrounded them with a full bucket in each hand was a delicate matter. One bucket held household slops, and the other, grain. To add spice to the adventure, the pigs — six of them, each weighing in the neighborhood of two hundred pounds — made a game out of seeing whether they could upset the buckets before I got them to the troughs. From experience, I can testify that the last thing one wants to do is sit down on an electrified fence when burdened with two bucketfuls of food and six hungry pigs.

Occasionally I would try to sneak up on them so that I could finesse the fence before they got there, but they seemed able to smell food when it was being scraped off plates in the kitchen. Next I tried diversion. Pigs are infinitely curious, and if you chuck an object like a rock into their pen, they will crowd around it, tasting and rooting until they are satisfied that it isn't edible, which allows the farmer time to negotiate the fence. But being clever, they soon catch on, and now the best a rock will draw is a reconnoitering scout. The ploy of spilling a little grain off to the side had the same history. Now, once they spot the bucket, they never take their eyes off it.

This particular afternoon I tried speed. I rounded the corner of the garden going, as they so aptly phrase it locally, straight out. Running flat out like that is difficult to do with two full buckets and the ghosts of prior failures to haunt you. The pigs were midway across their acre-sized pen when they spotted me, but they broke into an instant gallop, determined to make up for the head start I had. I had the feeling as I cleared the shin-high fence that we were like two berserk locomotives heading towards each other on a one-way track.

For once I won. I dropped the pail of slops and dumped the one with grain into the trough. The first pig to arrive never even gave me a glance, and he had his nose in the grain before I could put the bucket down. The rest followed suit, and I stood back panting, but satisfied.

Unless ill, pigs are dedicated eaters, and as I watched the contented curl of six tails, I decided that there was no better time than now to try out the fabled piece of baling twine. "PigpigpigNICEpigpigpig," I crooned as I took the twine from my pocket, made a girth hitch, and walked up on them. They took no notice of me as I bent over slowly, lifted one engrossed pig's leg, and slipped the noose in place.

I'm not sure what I expected, but absolutely nothing happened. The pig would occasionally shake its leg in the same way it would if it were being pestered by a fly. The third time it shook, I saw that the noose was slipping down the tapered leg, so I applied a little more tension. That did it. With a startled snort, he looked back over his shoulder and then danced to the side. In the process, he trampled two sisters on his right. One of the sisters bolted in alarm — right toward me.

Mimicking the tethered pig, I danced to the side, but this tightened the twine. With an alarmed squeal, the tethered pig decided I was the source of danger and spun to face me. A four-foot length of twine is not very long, and I found my hand in uncomfortable proximity to the scared pig's mouth. As a consequence, I matched the pig's spin by moving to get behind him. It was no use. The pig insisted on facing me, and I found myself running at the bitter end of the string like a tetherball.

When I finally realized I could release the twine, I was in my second circumnavigation. I must have been at the apogee of the orbit, for when I let go, I was running so fast that I was having trouble keeping my feet under me. Like a football player tripping through an obstacle course of old tires, I avoided the trough and the waterer but stepped directly into the slops bucket. From there it was only a hop, skip, and a jump to land on the electric fence.

Had Newton ever been able to see a man levitate off a live electric fence, he would never have been able to concoct his first law of gravity. Brushing the leftover pesto and spaghetti off my trousers, I retired to contemplate the evil forces afoot in the world that would kink the mind of an otherwise normal-seeming merchant like Seth Thomas. Reluctantly I concluded that Seth should not be singled out. In the future I will trust no one who suggests pulling someone else's leg.

17

BUT SOME KINDS OF TRUST are essential, especially in a rural circumstance. Remoteness and a severe climate make us more dependent on each other than our city cousins. Rural dependency carries a unique risk and trust: risk of our inner selves, and trust that our neighbors will use us right. For the most part, we have found our risk and trust to be justified. More important, we have found it returned.

After coming from the radical activism of Berkeley in the sixties, I found it unbelievable that I could be so nervous the first time I spoke at town meeting. Obviously, stating your views in any public gathering is scary because you risk rejection. But why, I asked myself at the time, should I feel more risk here in this little gathering than I did with larger groups in the city? The answer, I discovered, is that in the larger city gatherings I risked rejection of my views, but here I risked rejection of my views and of *myself.*

It came as a shock to me at a more recent town meeting, when I stood up to move a larger appropriation for the library, that I knew nearly everyone in that room better than I knew some of my closest city acquaintances; that somehow, without my consciously knowing it, my country neighbors had become friends whose approval I wanted.

I moved the agenda item that I had placed in the town warning (a booklet containing the meeting's agenda and reports from town officers) in a shaky voice and then sat down to look surreptitiously about me. Parsee Parsons — good 'ol Parsee — seconded the motion; Harry and Edna Whatcher sat immobile, their faces set; Noah Slack looked thoughtful; Perley Whitman frowned as Joy cuffed the littlest Whitman; Tom Roberts was on the edge of his chair while Mary sat back looking placidly happy with the third trimester of her pregnancy; and Vern The Pig Man whuffled Charlie Daniels into a semistuporous state. Seth Thomas's sonorous voice carried as he asked Mabel McIndoe if she had gotten the motion down in her clerk's notes.

"Mr. Chairman," squeaked Freddy McIndoe.

"Oh Gawd!" gargled Aaron Slack in an agonized stage whisper. "Freddy'll carry on 'til the cows come home!"

Seth is probably as impartial a moderator as we could have at town meeting, but being the general store owner, he also knew the foibles of his audience better than anyone else. He once said to me, "Freddy's all right. He just has more foibles than most of us."

Seth is said to keep a mental set of dossiers on every soul in town which, were they published, would make Saint Peter feel inadequate. He first tried to ignore Freddy's bantylike figure, but when no one else sought the floor, he tiredly acknowledged him.

"Fer years now," began Freddy adamantly, "we bin

eatin' too high off the hog! Raisin' the library's budget is bein' just plain piggy!"

Vern The Pig Man snorted indignantly.

Freddy's whiny clichés caused bored examination of fingernails and lengthy contemplation of the water stains on the meeting hall ceiling. "There's ee-sen-shuls," droned Freddy, "and there's whipped cream toppin'. Sooner'r later we got t'pay the fiddler." Eyelids began to quiver and droop. "What good're more books in the library," queried Freddy rhetorically, "when we can't get around decently on our town ruds?"

Under the thrumming, high whine of Freddy's voice my mind wandered ahead to the prospect of balmy days and mosquito bites. The deliciously warm days of summer almost justified the mosquitos, I decided. Only peripherally conscious of a nagging profundity in the thought, I allowed idyllic images of summertime to play across the screen of the inside of my eyelids . . . fields of timothy, their seed heads still in the boot, waving rhythmically under the urging of afternoon zephyrs . . . an unkindness of ravens disturbed at their carrion meal, cawing stiff-legged, wing-beating up from the hot tar surface of the road . . . a drift of hogs sporting in an open field.

". . . Y'can't bank a book," continued Freddy, "and y'can't replace a warshed out culvert with magazine subscriptions . . ."

I yawned as my thoughts continued their random course, and I twisted at the pages of the town warning. I remembered driving to the meeting and the pleasure I had felt as I watched the watery rush of snow-melt at the roadside. As I got out of the car, I recalled the fecund smell of swelling buds on the popples and the dopplering calls of chickadees that were now freed from dependence on winter feeders. Each year was the same. It was a time to contemplate the promise of a dark, wet earth which seemed to heave and swell with procreativness, and to be awed by the mystery of the black ponds as they shed their icy scales. It was a time to greet folks with clichés about the winter just past, and to share speculations about the outcome of the spring sugaring.

Several town meetings had passed since I had called this town home, and each one was a source of wonder to me. Yet again, I wondered at my wonder. Was it simply the eternal miracle of nature's renewal that happened each year at this time, or was it the town meeting itself? The first year I had been cynical about the success of any democratic institution as hoary and archaic as this, but over the years, this had progressively given way to grudging respect and finally, to admiration and growing committment.

I recalled a conversation I once overheard between Burger McIntosh and Noah Slack as they stood outside the hall during a recess from a particularly heated debate. Drawing on his Scottish roots, Burger observed heatedly, "I dinna ken these people. They go aboot the toown's business as though they each held a seat in the Hoose a Loorrds!"

"Yup," retorted Noah thoughtfully. "It does seem a fur piece t'go to git 'round puttin' up with thet Queen!"

In our own ways, Burger and I shared immigrant status in Vermont, and both of us had to make changes to cope with the harsh climate and sometimes irrascible local populace. As a farmer of strawberries and pigs, my initial cockiness was soon ground down by the whetstone of farming experience, and I rapidly learned the neccesity of slowing my pace to match the rural rhythms.

". . . Sure, we've got a little extra money in the town till," continued Freddy's remorseless voice as he broke into my mental meanderings, "but that doesn't mean that we have to pig out on it!"

Pigging out: to eat to satiety in unceremonious fashion. That, I ruminated, would be an apt dictionary definition of Freddy's metaphor — providing dictionaries included the term. Certainly pigging out conjured up colorful images for me, and I stole a look about me to see how it was received by those nearest me. I needn't have worried. Charlie Daniels was oblivious to Vern The Pig Man's periodic elbowings and was now snoring ostentatiously; Vern was staring with glazed eyes out through the wire mesh that had been installed over the windows to protect against errant basketballs when the meeting hall was used as a gym. Sal Burnstein was playing finger games, "This is the church, this is the steeple . . ." with his youngest; and Noah Slack's chin was doing jerky push-ups off his chest.

Freddy's voice was beginning to rub my nerves raw, and I had the impulse to rise, as parliamentarians phrase it, to a point of order — anything to stop that remorseless whining. Fortunately, my better sense prevailed. Town meeting goers give short shrift to picky parliamentarians. Besides, I rationalized, maybe, just maybe, Freddy had a point. Like the necessity of mosquitos in summer, maybe there was a corresponding need for Freddies in town meetings.

I bit my tongue and thought hard on that. Unbidden, the memory of standing in line at the IGA and overhearing Betsy Brockman defend Freddy to Edna Whatcher came to me. "He's kinda cute," simpered Betsy, whom everyone knew was a lonely widow who hankered after anything in long pants. "Granted he's small, but Freddy's got a good head on'm. I think he kinda grows on you."

"So does a pimple," returned Edna.

I bit harder. There had to be, I chastised myself, some reason for the Freddies of the world to exist. Sweat broke out on my forehead with the effort.

". . . We all pay our taxes, and we 'spect'm t'be spent
so's all of us benefit, not jest some'f us." He stared hard
at me. "And so, Mr. Moderator, I would urge everyone
t'vote no on this piggish library appropriation," concluded
Freddy. In the ensuing silence you could hear the ash floor-
ing pop as it contracted in the unaccustomed warmth of
the town's new oil furnace.

A sigh of relief swept the hall as Seth gratuitously
rapped his gavel and cleared his throat. "Siddown Parsee,"
he grated. "Freddy didn't make any motion that needs a
second."

Red-faced, Parsee resumed his seat, and everyone
laughed.

"Any further discussion?" asked Seth. "Mr. Schwenke
. . . Mr. Schwenke!"

"Yes?" I croaked as I shook off my reverie.

"Would you care to make any further defense of your
motion?"

I rose reluctantly and confronted the expectant, now-
familiar faces. Town meeting goers were a notoriously fickle
audience. They abhorred long-windedness, but they liked
a show, or at the very least, a reasonably cogent statement
having an honest ring to it.

The depression of my earlier unresolved ruminations
still hung on me, and I began with a rote defense of the
library's needs. Midway through a citation of the circula-
tion figures, I suddenly discovered that the nervousness that
had afflicted me at the beginning of the meeting had
dropped away. I wrapped up my rebuttal: "I agree with
Freddy when he says that we have to recognize that there
is a limited amount of wherewithall in the public trough,
but . . . ." Pausing for effect, I returned Freddy's stare. "But,
as a pig man I know that there has to be room at that trough
for everyone."

My presentation was not particularly inspired. It was probably merely adequate, but it did the job. Seth called for a routine voice vote, and there was not a nay vote to be heard. The issue was soon forgotten as the weight of other town business rapidly absorbed us, and it was not until the traditional self-congratulatory applause sounded at the end of the meeting and we were leaving the hall, that Freddy McIndoe reminded me of his earlier opposition.

"Nothin' personal in that library appropriation," he said as he cornered me in the hall's ancient cloakroom.

"I understand," I replied uncomfortably. In my experience, it was not like Freddy to mend fences.

"It's just that folks need t'be reminded that money's easy to give away, but it's allus hard t'come by."

"I guess," I mumbled, trying to see a way past him.

"Someone's gotta look after the town's pocketbook."

"Yeah," I replied spiritlessly, and with a sudden inspiration, I opened my battered copy of the town's warning. I flipped through to the tax collector's report and scanned the list of delinquent taxpayers. Sure enough, there were ten listings of properties owned by Frederick and Mabel McIndoe, all with delinquent taxes. "Yeah," I repeated as I drew out a pen, circled those properties, and tucked the warning in Freddy's coat pocket.

He was still fumbling at the folder in his pocket and staring at me dubiously as Mabel loomed alongside and took him into tow.

Because the meeting ran late, it was dark before we finally got home, and I had to turn on the light in the barn to do my chores. Amid the soothing smells and sounds of a nighttime barn, I sorted through my impressions of the day's happenings. The chickens murmured quietly as I picked up the eggs, put feed in the feeder, renewed the water, and spread some sawdust under their roost. By the time I had finished the job, I realized why I had lost my earlier nervousness before the meeting. The fact was that I had lost my self-consciousness and fear by becoming totally and honestly involved in the community's affairs.

It was not until I had put moistened feed into the new piglets' trough that I stumbled onto another significant truth to emerge from the meeting. As I watched the piglets' singular devotion to their food, I remembered Freddy's public admonition against pigging out. The pigs' squirming enthusiasm and youthful verve resurrected the excitement of the morning when I had looked about me and celebrated the arrival of spring.

It was, I decided, good to be here in this place, to be beginning again, to be alive. For whatever reason we are put here to suffer or to savor, this is *it*, and we need to prize it, nourish it, pig out on it, for unlike spring, it will not come round again. This place, right here and now, is hog heaven, and those who believe will sprout wings and fly.

18

The time has come, the walrus said,
To talk of many things,
Of shoes and ships and sealing wax,
Of cabbages and kings.
And why the sea is boiling hot —
And whether pigs have wings.

Alice in Wonderland

WHAT HARM CAN IT DO to suspend disbelief — for one moment to believe that pigs could sprout wings? Fantastic? Perhaps, but without fantasy we are all lost.

I am convinced that pigs too have a fantasy life. Last summer's litter included a little female who thought she was a diva. Appropriately, we named her Miss Piggy. She was aloof, finicky about her food, and had an astonishing variety of squeals, grunts, and wails that roamed irritatingly up and down the scale. As a piglet it was amusing, but her noise soon began to pall. Even her brothers and sisters grew to dislike her constant musicianship.

She would begin when the sun came up with a series of squeals that ascended the scales and then gradually shift over to purposefully spaced oinks that sounded uncannily like words. At first we thought she was sick, and on two occasions we called in Burger. On his last visit he pronounced her well and suggested sarcastically that she was singing Wagnerian lieder. His offhanded remark stuck with us, and after listening with more critical ears, we concluded that it was not lieder, but recitatives from various operas.

Even when she grew to be a big hog, we still called her Miss Piggy, the diva. There was little else we could do. She projected her fantasy with such piglike conviction that we were forced to acknowledge it. I fully expected to come out to the pen one day and find her on her hind legs, front legs clutched to her full bosoms delivering herself of Brünnhilde's sendoff of Siegfried "Zu neuen Thaten."

Joy Whitman, Perley's wife, was kind of like that. She wasn't an opera diva, or even a country music star. In fact, I think I can honestly say that she had a memorably bad voice. Folks even say that she was responsible for Betsy Brockman, one of our best singers, hanging around the local gin mill late on Thursday nights. It's Thursday nights when the North Kingdom Chorus meets for rehearsal. Joy and Betsy stand right next to each other in the soprano section, and I was seated in the front pew last Christmas when the chorus sang the Messiah, so I could clearly see Betsy's knees buckle when Joy hit a particularly spectacular off-key note.

No, Joy's fantasy wasn't along musical lines. In fact, I'm not sure what her fantasy was — nor was it, I think, important to know. What struck me when I first met Joy was my feeling that she was onto something, something big, something secret. Most everyone around town agreed. "That girl's going to go places!" they would say.

What the spark was, no one seemed willing to say. Certainly she exuded a mature confidence that was misplaced on her mere seventeen years. While she was unusually trim, she was not what one would call beautiful, nor was she especially brainy. But there was a competent feeling about her, a sense that she knew who she was, and, more important, who she would become. It was, therefore, a considerable surprise to everyone when she married Perley Whitman. She wasn't even pregnant when they took their vows. Perley was all right, but he wasn't what one would call a world beater.

From the beginning of their marriage they were in financial hot water. For a while they managed to make do with Joy staying home, but the struggle made its mark on Joy. When I would see her at the IGA during these hard times, I got the impression that she had put her fantasy, whatever it was, on hold.

Then she got pregnant. I went with Sue to the shower that was held for her. Local baby showers are barbaric affairs where women (I was the only male present) come with a gift for the pregnant one, and the recipient sits in the center of a ring made up of the donors while the showered one opens each gift with appropriate ohs and ahs. Their hands encumbered with coffee and cake, the donors are forced to make mental notes of who gave what, and how much each gift must have cost.

At best, baby showers around here try everyone, and while Joy's swollen body was there participating, her fantasy was not. The sparkle in her eyes was diminished to a faint glow as she said, "Oh, you dint need to do that, Joanne . . ."

When things got to be too much, Joy went to work in the local sweatshop making flimsy women's shoes to supplement Perley's starvation wages at the pulp mill. She took time off her job (unpaid) when she had her second kid, and while I did not attend the inevitable shower, I did see her with Perley at the local truck stop restaurant a year or so later. I hardly recognized her.

Her eyes were opaque and lusterless, and she had grown so fat that the drooling baby in her lap appeared to be merely another roll of flab on her belly. Though my stop to visit was mercifully brief, it was painful. The fantasy was gone, absolutely vanquished. In a mere five years the trim girl with the vision of the future had become an obese woman with her mind buried in the local graveyard of lost dreams.

Seeing Joy like that reminded me of Miss Piggy. Standoffish as that pig was, I always felt that she understood me when I talked to her. Maybe there was an element of condescension in her listening, but when I would cajole her to come and eat with the rest of her brothers and sisters, she would, eventually, ever so reluctantly, comply.

It was because of this sense of communication that I feel so guilty about Miss Piggy. The week before she was to be sent to the slaughter house I was doing routine maintenance work about the pen, and I offhandedly mentioned the fate that awaited her and her littermates. The following day I noticed something was amiss around the pigpen, but I couldn't put my finger on it. It wasn't until evening chores that I finally identified what it was.

Miss Piggy had forsaken her diva ways: no more recitatives, no more prolonged scale squeals, no more finicky eating. Her fantasy, as I sensed it, was dead. Overnight she had become . . . just another pig.

19

THERE WAS ONLY ONE PIG moving in the field. It was
the smallest boar. He was rooting somewhat aimlessly,
moving from a patch of pigweed to a clump of kale. His
brothers and sisters were scattered around the fenced-in
acre in various states of sybaritic ease. The largest sow had
rooted herself a long trough that was deep enough to
discover the wetter, cooler subsoils, and she lay flat on her
belly with her hind legs thrust out behind her. Her three
smaller sisters lay in the shade of the shelter I had provided,
and they were arrayed like jackstraws. The largest boar lay
submerged in the wallow he had created at the foot of the
demand waterer.

From my rocker on the porch, I watched the shim-
mering, Indian summer heat waves rise in somniferous pat-
terns that blended the pigs with their background. Like
the pigs, I was simply pleased to be alive, to have no other

purpose than to loll and absorb the decadent smells and
flaming colors of our New England fall.

But to young pigs, merely being alive is not enough.
The littlest boar was soon sated with inactivity. He approached his bigger sister and snuffled her snout. It was
clearly an invitation to play, but his sister was having none
of it. She lazily lifted one eyelid, whuffed once, and drifted
back into her ear-flapping sleep.

In frustration, the boar plowed a circling furrow with
his snout and came to an abrupt, dirt-tossing, spraddle-
legged stance right in front of her. She responded by turning her back on him and giving a long, sleepy sigh as she
melted into the cool earth. Undeterred, he inserted his
snout under her hindquarters and bounced her up and
down. Pleased with the irritable snorts he achieved for his
pains, he redoubled his efforts.

The action finally drew the attention of the other pigs.
I saw two white half-moons in the muddy mask that was
the bigger boar's face, and the three sisters' ears were
pointed in the direction of the disturbance as they began
to stir.

Despite her brother's sustained pestering, big sister
seemed determined to have her midafternoon nap, and the
little boar was forced to resort to the ultimate tease: he
chewed on her tail. She rose with an indignant squeal and
confronted her tormentor. Placing her rooter against his
chest, she gave him a heave that made his stubby hind legs
windmill as he sought to return to the fray. Jowl to jowl,
matching squeal for squeal, they engaged in mock battle.

It was all too much for the siblings. With anxious grunts
they clambered to their feet and began trotting toward the
whirling pigs. The largest boar, his white coat completely
obliterated with mud, was the first to arrive, and he wasted
no time with spectator kibitzing. He lowered his rooter

and ran headlong into his big sister's hindquarter, knocking her sideways. With a whinnying squeal, she regained her feet and charged an unsuspecting sister.

This began the game that we call pig tag, where the butting is passed on, one pig to another, until they are all involved in a melee. Hog wild, they charge and countercharge while keeping up the appearance of rage with their high-pitched squeals. Then suddenly, one of the participants gives the universal alarm call, a blend of a *whuff* and an *ungff*. Instantly all action ceases, and they freeze in an alert tableau, ears cupped forward, snouts to the wind, and tails twitching. If it were a real emergency, they would crowd their rear ends together and face outward, to the source of the danger.

But this is obviously play time. Gradually one of the pigs will lower his head as though he had lost something on the ground before him — I call this one the starter. Like his counterpart on the racetrack, his job is to startle the racers who are poised on their marks into flat-out speed.

Harf! snorts the starter, and the race is on. A racing pig is a thing of beauty, and I've often thought that racing circles missed something by not putting Porsche racing stripes on a porcine model. Ears flat back, they accelerate from zero to fifteen in two seconds flat, and in full stride, they are the epitome of streamlined Juggernauts. Pigs are dashers, not marathoners, and while at top speed, their bodies seem to travel dead level, like menacing torpedoes. But they lose their threatening aspect as they slow.

Their racing gait soon shifts down to a gallop that has a unique rocking horse motion, then slower through a single-foot, into a trot, and finally, to a walk. The latter signifies that the game is over, and they fan out. Their sides heave with their exertion, and up on the porch, I can hear them wheeze and cough as they seek shade or a little refreshment at the waterer.

There is a companionable feel around the pigpen following a romp, and the mellowness matches the smell of burning leaves that perfumes the autumnal air. The muddy big boar joins two of his sisters who have sought the creeping shade of a butternut tree. They root briefly and then altogether collapse into a pile in the resulting declivity. The larger sow and a smaller sister quibble briefly at the waterer as to who is to go first, and then both settle down simultaneously for a long protracted soak in the healthful mud of the spa.

Soon all that moves is the smallest boar. He roots placidly about the periphery of the electric fence, moving with increasing restlessness toward the pile of his siblings in the shadow of the butternut tree.

20

HARRY WHATCHER used to tell me, "A pig is just a young hog." There were a lot of negative vibes that came down with that dictum, and until I learned something about swine, I believed him. Actually raising pigs has shown me that this is akin to the nonsense espoused by some educators who say that a child is just a young adult. I contend that being a pig, or a child, is a state of mind.

In theory, a pig is a pig until it reaches 120 pounds, at which point it becomes a hog; a child becomes an adult at some magical date sixteen or eighteen years after birth, depending on what state he or she lives in. What could be more far-fetched?

One year Harry brought home a couple of piglets. I happened to be driving by at the time, and I stopped in amazement as he dumped the pigs into a no-nonsense pen, made of cyclone fencing, out behind the barn. My amazement stemmed from the fact that Harry is a dairy farmer, and as such, had always seemed to look down on pigs.

"How come?" I asked him while I helped haul water and feed.

"Can't get a decent pork chop," he answered tersely, "and Edna wants salt pork to go in her baked beans."

I didn't question any further. I knew that native Vermonters prized their salt pork (thick slabs of backfat that are pickled in brine), and that they did not put much store by the kind of bacon-style pigs that I raised. But my interest in Harry's project was more than academic. How, I wondered, would Harry cope with the trials that pig raising entailed. Harry has an unbending dignity that I had seen tested by fractious first-calf heifers, but pigs are something else, and I was looking forward to learning more, about pigs, or about dairymen who decide to raise pigs.

About Harry I did not learn much, other than the fact that he knew how to put up an impenetrable fence, and that he still did not particularly care for pigs. But about pigs, I learned a great deal. Harry's pigs did not put on weight very fast despite the fact that he shoveled milk and grain into them with mechanical regularity. Pigs are gregarious animals. Like children, they thrive on affection, enjoy toys, have a short attention span, and are easily bored. But other than to feed or water them, Harry rarely visited the remote pen. They were simply there.

From the moment they were dumped into the cyclone fence pen, Harry's pigs became hogs. Their world was instantly narrowed to each other, the food, and the sty, and as they grew, their world became smaller and smaller. The tedium of their existence soon became apparent: they were lethargic, exhibitted ragged ears, had droopy tails, and rapidly acquired that dull-eyed glaze that swineherds associate with six- or seven-year-old breeding hogs.

By comparison, the piglets that I had acquired at the same time grew at only a slightly slower rate, a difference I attributed to the quantities of milk that Harry fed. But otherwise, our pigs could not have been more different. My pigs' eyes were clear and inquisitively alert; their ears were whole and clean; and they carried their tails lifted in chase or curled in contentment. While my pigs accumulated weight and outwardly began to look like hogs, they remained piglike in their behavior right up until butchering day.

I never gave the pig comparison much more thought until one day when my daughter, Linda, came to visit. It was after supper, and in fatherly fashion I was attempting to convince her to think twice about her latest wild-eyed enthusiasm: she wanted to acquire a horse while living in a city suburb. I was about to launch into my clinching argument against the scheme when Harry and Edna stopped by with their daughter, Amy.

In the course of their visit I mentally stepped back from the polite conversation and found myself looking at the two kids with a calculating eye (as both were in their thirties, "kids" is a fatherly euphemism). Outwardly they were very much alike, but otherwise they couldn't have been more different. Amy was subdued, practical, and pacific; Linda was effervescent, wildly impractical, and rebellious.

As Harry and his family got into their car, Harry looked toward the pigs in the field. "Mighty thrifty lookin'," he said speculatively. I knew that he was comparing mine with his own.

"Thanks," I said with a smile. Surreptitiously I slipped Linda a dollar bill and whispered, "You can apply this to that nag you aim to get, but I still think you're madder than a March hare."

To Harry I added generously, "I can raise pigs, but I reckon you raise better hogs."

21

COMPARING KIDS AND PIGS is mucking around on dangerous ground. If you think I exaggerate, consider the case of my neighbors and friends, Kim and Bob Grey. Recently a photojournalist from a national publication visited their farm, and in the course of recording his visit on film, photographed Kim moments after she had captured an errant piglet. At the time, Kim was wholesomely eight months pregnant, and the snapshot showed the squealer in her arms with its tiny hooves resting on her protruding belly.

The picture became the cover of the publication, and the controversy began. Nationally, opinion seemed equally divided. Some wrote saying that Kim was beautiful (she is), and that juxtaposing her with the little porker was delightful. Others (all women) said, "poor taste," "offensive," "(pregnancy is) private and personal and should be shown or depicted with all respect." One aggitated soul from Massachusetts wrote, "This sends the message that women, as animals, are pleased to mother anything at all!"

Locally, things were considerably better, but what interested me was how the pros and cons split. The minority, folks who were against the photograph, were predominantly women who were either heavily into religion or newcomers who had never raised animals — sometimes they were both. Their objections were much the same as those expressed by correspondents to the publication.

A child *in utero* is close to a woman's heart (literally, about four inches), and a sensitivity to the issues surrounding pregnancy, though not definitive, is understandable. In our town the women outnumber the men. We have double the national average of retired people, and because most women outlive their spouses, the retirement community is largely made up of elderly women. There are few social outlets in Newbury; therefore, it is no surprise that these elderly women make up the backbone of the local churches.

But age is not a clinching factor. I showed the magazine cover to Betsy Brockman's mother, who, alongside her husband, farmed the top of Leighton Hill until he died. She said scornfully, "Any fool can see that that pig needed picking up. Someone weaned the little critter too early." And Edna Whatcher's daughter, Amy, was visiting from California when I showed her the cover. She allowed as how she missed "the old homestead" and then pointed to the earrings in Kim's ears as she said, "Those're nice. I wonder where she got them." In neither case did the women express any negative reaction to the juxtaposition of the piglet and Kim's pregnancy. And when I did call their attention to the controversy, they merely shrugged it off as "the mischief of idle minds."

I suspect that it narrows down to how and where you were raised. Most of the nonfarming newcomers come from large urban areas, and they tend to settle in one of Newbury's three tiny villages. They are regarded by anyone who has lived here for a while with knee-jerk xenophobic distrust or with wait-and-see reserve. The latter is the predominant reaction, and it has its roots in experience.

Generally, nonfarming newcomers came here for negative reasons: they migrated to "escape the rat race," or they came to "avoid the crime and corruption of the cities." Rarely do they ever come with the stated purpose of "starting a new career," or "beginning anew." Instead, after they have arrived, they can be heard in social gatherings as they carp about "the unreliability of the locals," or at town meeting where they air their inevitable complaints about "the lack of town services." In a rare moment of pique, Noah Slack once said to me, "these city folks're like blue-jays — they're flashy, yakkety, selfish, and they got pointed heads."

As a town father, Noah's observations deserve serious consideration, but in this case I think he came up short because of his weak bladder and the fact that he was in a thrash.

I heard a better analogy when our sow first threw a litter of eleven babies. That's a lot for a first litter, and I was apprehensive as I called Vern The Pig Man to come over for a consultation. Together we leaned on the wooden rails of our improvised farrowing pen and watched the parade of tiny bodies as they advanced on the sow's waiting teats. I was particularly intrigued by the first in line whom I had isolated by the large, liver-colored freckle in the middle of his back. I had watched him once before, and as on that previous occasion, he staggered past the entire array of teats to the farthermost end before plugging in. When I remarked on it to Vern, he explained, "Piglets will only suck off of one particular tit. To them it doesn't seem to matter that the frontward tits have more milk and the hind ones less. Once they get attached to a tit, there is no displacing them. They're like one-track-minded people who get stuck in a rut." He laughed. "The difference is that pigs grow out of their rut."

Probably I have made more of a do about these folks' response to Kim's cover picture than it deserves, but it grieves me to stand by helplessly while they blindly act out a tragic, self-fulfilling prophecy. Downcountry people, for example, are drawn by the open spaces and the slow rhythms of rusticity of our town, but many find that they cannot abide the solitude or the slow pace of the country after they get here. Like pigs who determinedly eat themselves into butchering condition, these newcomers set about altering the local circumstances to fit the city mold from which they fled. If they succeed, they then bemoan the loss of their country ambiance.

But we all make our own ruts. For example, when I showed the controversial picture to Harry Whatcher, his first reaction was, "She's one of the new folks in town, ain't she?"

There was no mistaking the reserve in his voice, and I responded, "The Greys're new here, but they're native Vermonters."

Harry visibly relaxed. "That so? . . . She looks like a worker."

From Harry this was high praise. The Puritan work ethic still runs strong amongst local people, and by saying that she had the look of a worker, Harry was quietly stating a sweaty rut that has been acquired, nurtured, and universally shared by his peers.

These ruts run deep, and no one, whether they come from the city or the country, avoids them. Like my sow, the country has "milk" enough for everyone, but some of us piglets seem bound and determined to suck the "hind tit."

22

IT WAS A HOT AND HUMID AFTERNOON, and big black clouds were building to the south. For the third time this summer I was replacing the facer board on the pigs' trough. They seemed to regard it as a teething ring or a rigid piece of dental floss. I looked up as I heard Tom Roberts's tractors pulling onto the field just south of ours. The place next door had recently changed hands, and the new summer folks were glad to have Tom mow their "lawn."

This forenoon, after the morning's dew had evaporated, Mary Roberts had tedded the hay, and now it was ready to rake and bale, providing they got it done ahead of the upcoming storm. From the high-pitched revs of the tractor engines I knew that Tom and Mary were aware of the race, and I put in the last nail with a sigh. I still had a lot of chores to get done before the rains, but . . . .

As I put away my tools I watched the low stoop of the barn swallows and the pigs' nervous snuffling. Both were sure signs that the rains were not far away, and I began to hurry. I called Sue, and she put aside the peas that she was shelling to join me. Crossing our field we watched the spoor of Mary's rake being frantically sniffed up by Tom's baler and deposited in rectangular droppings, and we climbed through the barbed wire fence to welcoming "hallos" and "what keptchas?"

Even if you could be heard above the roar of the tractors and the monotonous *kachunckakachunk* of the baler, there wasn't any need for conversation. I went over to Tom's old ton-and-a-half Ford stakeside, started it up, and bumped my way over the slanty hillside to a spot midway between a lot of bales. As I set the handbrake and got out, I could see the new summer folks up on their brand new deck. Arrayed on their color-coordinated loungers in madras shorts and white polo shirts, they made a splash of color against the weathered sides of the old Peavy house.

Wearily we began gathering bales and tossing them up on the flatbed of the truck. The heat was oppressive, and we soon began to sweat, which, in turn, made the chaff stick to our arms. As I worked I recalled the one conversation I had had with my new neighbors. They had bought the place, they said, so that their kids, two sulky teenage boys, could, as they had put it, "experience the country." When I suggested that perhaps the boys might want to hire out to clean the manure from the pen where I had kept the pigs when they were younger, they collectively looked at me as though I had belched in the midst of a diplomatic reception line.

Sue interrupted my reverie with a whistle, and I looked in the direction she was pointing. Noah and Perley had just gotten out of Perley's new pickup, which he had carefully parked in the shade of a big maple, and were headed our way. Noah glanced up at the threatening clouds as he shouted, "We ain't got nawthin' better t'do!" and he began pitching bales with a strength that belied his years.

With Sue stacking we began to make better progress, and I moved the truck farther up the field. Distant rumbles of thunder spurred us on, and I watched from under sweat-beaded eyebrows the errant gusts of wind that shook the popples on the edge of the field. I never saw him arrive, but suddenly Parsee Parsons was alongside me lugging two bales of hay that weighed almost as much as he did. "Jest happenin' by," he grunted as he threw first one and then the other in Sue's direction.

When the baler quit, the storm seemed instantly closer. The rumbles of thunder began to take on individual definition, and we could make out the onrush of each billow of wind as it sped northward through the sugar bush. Without comment, Mary took over driving the truck, and Tom helped Sue stack the rapidly accumulating hay.

"Now that," said Perley with unfeigned envy as he pointed towards the summer folks, "is the way to live!" Sweat made rivulets through the chaff on his forehead, and he was panting with the exertion of throwing bales four-high on the truck.

"Beats workin'," gasped Parsee as he struggled to hold a bale that hadn't made it to the top.

I glanced up to the house just as the woman, trim and sensual in her cut-off shorts, emerged with a trayful of drinks. I must have stared extra long, for Sue dropped a bale of hay on my head.

"Only way I could get that horsefly that was chewing on your ear," she giggled. Adeptly she ducked my flying riposte.

The claps of thunder began to have a snap to them as

we threw the last of the bales onto the truck and covered our treasure with a tarp. Up at the house the summer folks gave up their grandstand seats as the first drops fell.

Mary and Tom headed for the barn with a lot of waving and yelling, and we scattered for the cover of the pickups. Sue and I hopped in with Noah and Perley, and in the course of the short, steamy drive to our dooryard, the skies turned so dark that Perley had to turn on his headlights, and the squally shower overtaxed the truck's wipers.

"Makes you wonder how anybody gets anything done in this country, doesn't it?" I asked thinking of my pig chores.

Noah grinned at me and said, "Shoot boy, this is jest the shank of the evenin'!"

23

"HOW CAN YOU SAY that working is fun?" demanded Sym Tamaleo incredulously.

It was one of those dog days of summer, and I was uprooting the pea vines from the garden to feed to the pigs while Sym followed me around. Sym, his given name was Franco, had come to make a quick pitch for my vote and had stayed for an hour — so far.

"I didn't say that working is fun for everyone," I corrected him. "I only said that I enjoyed working."

Sym did not appear happy with the correction. He took out a spotlessly clean handkerchief and mopped his brow. It was hot in the midday sun, and the humidity had long ago forced him to shed his light sportscoat and loosen his tie. "Maybe this sweaty life is all right for you," he argued with a hint of truculence, "but you weren't brought up here."

That didn't appear to warrant comment, so I held my tongue. I finished untangling another row of vines from the supporting pea fence and began pulling them and throwing them into the wheelbarrow. The pigs loved the peas if they were not all browned over or whitened with mildew. As I worked, I thought about the years that I had lived on and had worked this farm. They had been lean years, years when it had been hard to hold things together and still pay the taxes — the same taxes that Sym used to pay for the gas to motor out here to tell me that I should be honored, even though I hadn't been brought up here. But they had been good years, ones that left me tired enough to sleep nights, even muggy nights like those of the past week.

"Young folks born around here should know that there are alternatives out there," continued Sym, waving at the ether. "They need to be told that they don't have to stick around this dump, that they don't have to end up poor and stove-in from a lifetime of overwork."

I didn't know Sym very well — he came around once before when he ran against that Bible thumper from Groton — but having endured his reports at town meeting of the goings-on in the state legislature, I had the feeling that he was just getting wound up. I picked up the oiled handles of the heaped wheelbarrow and started for the field where we kept the pigs. Hands on hips, coat slung in an elbow, Sym dogged my boot tracks.

"Hell," I heard him say behind me, "most newcomers in town are annuity hippies or kids who are being staked by their rich downcountry parents. They don't know what it means to have to work to buy a place."

I had heard this line often enough before. Like all popular clichés, there was a kernel of truth in it, and it allowed the user to feel like he was part of a knowledgeable majority. The last time I had heard it was from Harry Whatcher, moments after he had told me how he had inherited his farm.

But Sym had a point. He had been born here, and I had not. Maybe, I thought, some ambitious jingoist of the future will propose that natives like Sym get an extra half vote for merely being indigenous. But then Harry Whatcher would complain that his four generations were not accorded their proper respect, and that he should wield at least three votes.

"Why on earth do you want to get reelected to the state legislature, Sym?" I asked as I unloaded the wheelbarrow.

"What do you mean?"

"Well, folks say that you're interested in running for the lieutenant governor's job over to Montpelier." I didn't need to look at him to know that he was eyeing me calculatingly.

More than one politician had hung himself by saying too much too early, and he already knew that he owed the origins of his nickname, Sym, to the same grapevine that I was tuned in to. Sym, as Seth Thomas once told me, was short for "Slick Young Man." Noah Slack was standing alongside Seth at the time, and he added, "Folks've got Sym's number, the boy's ambitious and clever, but if'n you're smart, you don't bee-grudge cleverness in hosses or in polly-tish-uns."

"Well, I don't know about the lieutenant governorship," said Sym finally, "but who knows where a Catholic kid raised in the stone sheds of South Ryegate could end up."

As we stood watching the pigs barrelling across the open field for the peas, I couldn't help but wonder at the politician's ubiquitous need to exaggerate his plebian roots.

Everyone knew that it was Sym's dad, Rocco Tamaleo, who had worked in the stone sheds. The nearest Sym had come to them was as a kid when he played in the waste piles of grout. Rocco had come straight from Italy to the stone sheds of South Ryegate, where he had inhaled enough of the famous gray granites of Barre to finish the job that silicosis had begun in Italy.

"You should be happy that someone has already broken that old prohibition against a Catholic president," I said jokingly.

"Yes." Sym wasn't joking.

The pigs arrived in a cloud of dust and dove into the pile of pea vines that I had set out. Sym and I leaned on fence posts quietly sharing a countryman's enjoyment of their single-minded gluttony. The pile was soon demolished, and minor squabbles broke out as the pigs became sated and began to play with the food.

"Isn't that always the way it is . . . ," I observed in disgust, "with pigs, I mean." I stepped over the electric fence and cleared the trampled remainders so that they would not foul the fence.

Sym looked at me sharply. "Yeah, I guess it is."

The temptation to deliver myself of a homily on hunger and satiation, pigs and politicians, was almost more than I could bear. But in an insightful moment, one that is all too rare in my case, I realized that it would be wasted. If there was any one single, valuable lesson that I had learned from living and tending pigs in Vermont, it is that it rarely pays to try to "run" people or pigs.

"Well, I guess I'd better be peedling along," said Sym. "Can I count on your vote this year?"

"Unless someone better comes along," I answered promptly.

It was a typical Vermont answer, and Sym responded

with a smile. "Funny, that's exactly what my wife said when I asked if she'd have me."

I waved as his car turned at our mailbox and watched as he disappeared up the road. His noisy exhaust receded, and gradually the real sounds began to return. From the basswood over my head came the buzz of our bees making honey, and a ratchety woodpecker worked a telephone pole in the distance. Behind me, the huffling and harfing indicated that the pigs were beginning another of their interminable games of tag.

When I turned to watch their cavortings, I began to laugh with the joy of it all. They really knew how to live — while the living was good.

24

IT WAS A HUMDINGER of a fall Saturday. The early
morning frost had left diamonds of dew on the grass, and
the air bore the tangy aroma of overripe apples underlaid
with the earthy smell of rotting leaves. As had been my
Saturday habit for the past six months, I started out to draw
a load of pig grain, and I was in good humor because I knew
that the pigs were almost butchering size, and this would
be the last trip for the year.

On the way to town, I was euphoric. I had the windows down and was singing along with a nasal redneck
on the local country music station when I passed the Haven
Rest Home. Perhaps it was the sight of two white-headed
ancients rocking on the front porch that squelched my high
spirits, but more likely it was my own guilty conscience.
Gideon Whitman had been an inmate — a guest? — of the
home for over a year now, and not once in all the times

I had driven by had I stopped to see him. Why, I wondered as I turned the radio off, did I avoid this contact? I had no ready answer, so I resolved to stop on my return trip.

Despite my resolution, I nearly bypassed the place again. As I approached the Haven Rest Home's parking lot, I suddenly realized why I had not stopped before. Death hung about that place like a work collar on a draft horse. The only other time that I had seriously confronted my own mortality was when I was a kid, barely out of my teens, in Korea, and then death was an impersonal chance throw of the dice. Here death was personal, its sentence as inexorable as a sunset. I was afraid.

It turned out that I had just cause for my fears. The old folks out on the lawns and on the porch were the bright spots of the Haven. Inside, the corridors were littered with old derelict people in wheelchairs, and they all had a curious sameness, an imploded look that gave their slow upward glances at my passing each an identical look into eternity. My stomach knotted as I got directions to Gideon's room and heel-clattered the length of an anonymous corridor. Each step added to my fear, and I shunted it off by accumulating and feeding an anger with Gideon's son, Perley, the same son that Gideon fourteen years before had so prized, the same son who had committed him to this place.

At the open door to Gideon's room, I excused myself as I stumbled over the foot of one of the wheelchair residents who was parked there. Smiling blankly at the nodding old man in the wheelchair, I was about to knock on Gideon's door when I saw the shiny chrome pig lying in his passive fingers. The last time I had seen that chrome pig it was mounted on the hood of Gideon's old, battered pickup.

"Gideon?"

The old man's head rose slowly, and once more I

looked unfocused into eternity. Then, ever so slowly, the man behind the eyes crossed back over the vale, and he licked his scaly, dry lips with a powdery tongue.

"Yesss?" The voice was as cracked and dry as his lips. "Who are you?" he asked querulously. Seeking comfort in the familiar, his gnarled hands caressed the chrome pig.

"It's Karl . . . Karl Schwenke. How are you, Gideon?"

Falteringly, "Karl Schwenke? Do I? . . . Oh yesss . . . my neighbor who raises pigs." His skeletal face twisted into a mockery of a smile. He held the shiny pig up for me to look at. "I really like pigs."

"You always were the best pig man in town," I said over the lump in my throat.

"Yesss . . . I was." Declarative statement, and again querelous, "Did you know . . ." Silence as he lost the thread. "Did you know that I'm dying, neighbor?"

My turn to be silent. "Yes," I answered finally. "We are all dying."

Again silence, and then an unlikely cackle burst forth from the frail old man's lips. "That's easy for you to say, you young bustard." He used the hem of his thin pajama top to polish the chrome pig and said fervently, "Goddemit, but it's good t'talk to a pig man again."

Then his head sank down against his bony breast, and for a moment I thought he had drifted off to sleep. "Did I ever tell you the one about the wild boar and the preacher?" he said into his chest. His voice was so faint I could barely hear him.

"No," I replied. He had, but I was willing to hear it again.

His head rose with an effort that made the cords on the back of his neck stand out like tractor treads, and his voice took on its old character as he began, "Back when folks in our town wuz still hackin' at the wilderness they wuz a circuit preacher come up from Boston t'baptize the heathen. He was stayin' with the Sawyer family over t'Topsham when Sawyer's old boar, who'd gone hog wild, ate the youngest Sawyer kid. Helleva stink. Lots of tooin' and froin' b'fore the funeral 'bout killin' that boar. But Sawyer wouldn't have none of it. 'Waste'f a good studdin' boar,' he says, 'and, anyways, it warn't the boar's fault.' And b'God he stuck to his guns.

"Wal mistah!" Gideon's interjection lacked its customary verve, and I could see the struggle that it took to go on, but I did not interrupt.

"First thing off folks was some upset, but they simmered down," he continued. "They mostly knew that a good studdin' boar was hard t'come by so they made some 'lowances, but that preacher wouldn't have none of it. He was fit t'be tied. He was 'a civilized man', he says, and he wasn't goin' t'live under the same roof as a man who thought so little of his kids.

"That night after the funeral the preacher packed up kit and kaboodle and was headin' out the door when Sawyer reminded him that the boar was runnin' loose in the dooryard. 'The Lord'll perteck the righteous,' says the preacher, and out he goes. Sawyer commenced t'feelin' guilty 'bout sendin' the preacher out into the dark, so he sent his oldest boy out with a lantern t'light the preacher's way. The boy no sooner caught up with the preacher than they spotted the boar standin' b'tween them'n the barn. By lantern light that boar's eyes looked like the devil's own, red and mean. As soon's the preacher saw that pig he sits right down and starts takin' off his shoes.''

At this point Gideon's voice faltered, dwindling away to a hoarse croak. The effort to tell the story taxed his weakened condition, and I found myself having to choke off the desire to deliver the punchline for him. I could not put my finger on how I knew, but I was dead certain that the telling was important to him.

His voice was weak, but steady as he went on, " 'Is it true what you said b'fore, that the Lord'll perteck the righteous?' asked the scared boy.

" 'He first pertecks the swift,' answered the preacher scramblin' to his feet.

" 'But you can't outrun that boar,' says the boy.

" 'I don't aim to,' says the preacher over his shoulder. 'I figure that all I got t'do is outrun you!' "

My laughter echoed hollowly in the corridor. Gideon managed only a wheeze, but his gaunt features were wrinkled in a parody of his usual grin. In the past he almost always laughed at his own pig stories, and I ached to hear his laughter now.

A passing nurse's aide looked at us strangely, and my laughter trailed away. Gideon had gone back to polishing the chrome pig with the tail of his pajamas.

"Is there anything I can get for you, Gideon? . . . Magazines? Newspapers? Books?"

He never looked up. "Nope, I reckon not," he said in a barely audible whisper. "But I'd consider it a favor if you'd take this . . ." He held out the shiny chrome pig without looking up at me. "This demned pig is a nuisance, and he needs t'be in the company of a pig man."

"Gideon, I can't . . ." My choked-up refusal died on my lips as he looked up at me pleadingly, and I took the pig with one hand and his cornhusk-dry hand with the other. "All right," I said, "and I'll keep it polished until you want it back."

"Suah," he breathed, and his eyes began to lose their focus. "Y'know," he said finally, "I really liked pigs."

It was on that note that I left the Haven Rest Home, and I never went back. It came as no surprise when Perley called Sunday morning to tell me that Gideon had died in his sleep the night before.

25

WE HAD SCHEDULED everything for the upcoming weekend very carefully. The itinerant butcher, Harley Black, had told us to bring the pigs in from the field and pen them in the barn preparatory to his arrival on Saturday. Because Sue's teachers' conference required that she be in Boston on Friday, and the conference would last through the weekend, we decided to move the pigs on Thursday.

Thursday dawned a beautiful fall day. It was slightly on the crisp side, but the air was clean and invigorating. After breakfast, everything seemed on the up side: the distance from the electrically fenced field to the barn was less than a hundred yards, we had ten years of experience with pigs, and we only had three pigs to move. Such is the eternal optimism of man.

Our weeder geese were working in our acre-sized

strawberry patch adjacent to the pigs when we came out, and they greeted us with their usual raucous chorus of *grief!* . . . *grief!* As we stood next to their fence planning our pig-moving strategy, the geese simmered down and satisfied their aggressive instincts with an occasional hissing, S-necked charge. Accustomed to being fed at this time, the three pigs were snuffling impatiently right at the fence, and they were taken aback when I reached down, disconnected the electric fence, and spread the wire back out of the way.

Twice during the summer they had defeated the electric fence by uprooting the posts on which the fence depended, and both times they went out over the grounded wire. Each taste of freedom found it more difficult to herd them back inside, and I reasoned that they would jump at this new opportunity. Instead they backed away with heads lowered and ears raised, and sniffed the breeze for threat from an unexpected direction. It is this kind of behavior that I believe prompted the expression, pig-headed.

A bucketful of grain helped. Soon the two sows were outside the fence, but the boar was not to be lured so easily. In fact, he was obviously not going to have anything to do with crossing the spot where the fence once stood, and as time and the grain in the bucket dwindled away, we saw the makings of a major problem.

Being social animals, pigs do not like to be separated, and the boar was already sounding the recall. A pig in an open field defies catching, so we decided to begin the migration toward the barn with the two sows, hoping that the boar would realize that he was in the minority and would join us. I couldn't believe it when it worked. After a lot of squealing protests as the sows followed the grain bucket, the boar crossed over the line and began to trail us.

It was a stop-and-go processional. Carefully crowding the panic distance — the physical space that pigs insist on maintaining — we herded the two pigs ahead of us. We each carried 2 five-foot herding sticks, which we extended periodically to indicate our increased sphere of influence. The sticks were also used occassionally for a judicious poke to keep an errant sow's head pointed in the right direction, or to prompt movement. Such, I told myself in a self-congratulatory manner, is the nature of pig herding, a careful balancing of quiet enticement, threat, and momentum.

Except for the trailing boar, it was a picture-book move. The sows required only one prod to step into the dark of the barn, and another to saunter into the waiting stall. Sue held the door as I went back for the boar.

He was standing spraddle-legged outside the barn door with his head lowered, and one eye cocked at me with an appropriately suspicious look.

It was clear to him that I was not returning his sisters, and he squealed another summons. I heard the answering squeals, the stall door slam, and Sue's warning that the sows had panicked. She would, she said, open the adjoining stall for the boar.

Whatever it was that the sows communicated to their misanthropic brother, it put his tail up. He spun about and began to retrace his steps at a steady trot. I tried to outpace him in a circling maneuver, but he kept a wary eye peeled on me and adjusted his trot accordingly. In no time we were back at the field. Discouraged, Sue joined me there, and together we reactivated the fence. Afterwards we stood staring balefully at the recalcitrant boar while we examined our alternatives. Prudence and a telephone call to Vern The Pig Man indicated that we should let hunger work for us, and we reluctantly abandoned the project for the day.

That night the boar seemed no more willing to cooperate than he had in the morning hours. A pail of grain got him as far as the fence and no farther. The next morning Sue left for Boston only after I assured her that if worst came to worst, I could leave the pig for the butcher, Black, to deal with.

In dealing with his fellow animals, pride is man's worst enemy. It is certainly mine. The thought of explaining my ineptitude to Black, a stranger, galled me. Sue was scarcely out of sight before I began building a pig crate on wheels. As the noon hour rolled around I wheeled my contraption out on the field. The boar alertly watched as I adorned the floor of my crate with apples and baited the ingeniously conceived deadfall trigger that would drop the crate's hinged door. When I retired from the field, I was looking forward to a cool bottle of homemade beer, and I was utterly confident of victory.

Four hours and six bottles of home-brew later, I concluded that the ruse was not going to work. With only the beer for solace, I spent the time on the porch watching with mounting irritation as the boar alternately chewed, scratched, and peed on my creation. Though he obviously wanted the apples, he steadfastly refused to step one trotter inside the crate. The crowning indignity came midway through my seventh bottle of beer, when the boar upended the whole affair and spilled the apples out where he could get them without fear of penalty.

It took a stern, if somewhat tipsy, exercise of willpower to keep from charging out on that field and chasing the cussed boar until he, or I, dropped from exhaustion.

"Guile!" I snarled aloud. "What I need is a little guile!" I slammed the bottle down on the porch railing, and the vehemence of the gesture splashed beer all over my knees.

I suspect that I will never know whether it was the smell of the spilt brew or the complaining squeal of the hungry boar that prompted the idea, but I was up in a wobbly trice and headed for the garden shed. The wheelbarrow seemed to float on air as I ran it from the shed to the kitchen door, and it only took a few weaving side trips to load it with the refrigerator's contents. Then, with an opener in my jeans and a dozen bottles of home-brew rattling in the bottom of the barrow, I wove a serpentine track down to the field.

Grief!. . . grief! honked the weeder geese pessimistically. I ignored them, opened the fence, and wheeled the barrow right up to the trough. The moment I hove into sight, the boar took himself to the opposite side of the field. Pointedly, I ignored him as I opened the first bottle and poured the contents into the trough.

No reaction.

I opened another and ostentatiously took a healthy swig before pouring the rest into the trough. The boar began to look interested. By the time I got to the eighth bottle I noted that the bottle opener was malfunctioning. Despite my best efforts, it would not center on the bottle caps, and when I finally did get it in position, it would repeatedly slip to the side.

The tenth bottle did it. I had to make a great show of how delicious it was by drinking half of it first, but piggish greed was on my side, and eventually the boar sidestepped up next to the trough and took a tentative sip.

"Boy, is that great stuff!" he said as he sucked up the brew.

I agreed, and employing the malfunctioning bottle opener on another bottle, toasted the success of the batch.

Grief! . . . grief! warned the geese.

26

IT WAS ALMOST TEN O'CLOCK and still no Harley
Black. He had warned me that this was his busy time of
year, and he had explained that he had another job to do
in the forenoon before he got to our place. That was no
excuse, I peeved. Over my eighth cup of black coffee, I
stared out bleakly at the slanty, sleety rain remembering
my painful predawn wakening.

Awareness had encroached on oblivion, like a tooth-
ache. I knew only that I was a wreck. It was pitch-dark,
a heaving, pounding dark. Groaning, I lifted the bloated
balloon that was attached to my shoulders and discovered
that the pounding earthquake was my bedmate's heartbeat.
Bed? Bedmate? My exploring hand found sawdust ...
sawdust? ... found a nose ... my nose ... good ol' nose
... smells! My God, I was in the barn!

Recollections of the previous day descended on my

throbbing head with all the delicacy of a rooster pouncing on a cowering hen. My enquiring hand encountered the boar's coarse-haired side. His even breathing indicated that he was still out like a light, but as I gingerly lifted my head, he gave out a piteous moan that renewed our soulmateness.

Woozily I rose and, careful not to disturb my drinking companion's peaceful slumbers, felt my way to the stall door. The stygian darkness was impenetrable, and the raised door sill defeated me. I tripped, and as I plunged forward, my already bruised shins remembered too late where I had left the wheelbarrow. I fetched up with an agonized bellow that would have done credit to a horny moose, and proceeded to hop about on one foot.

What with the consequent bedlam, the chickens' squawking, the two sows' alarmed harfing, and the distant geese's grief, griefing, it is understandable that I cannot remember the exact sequence of events that followed my progress around the darkened barn. But I think that the bloody nose came from the rake leaning against the stall rail, and that the enormous bruise on my buttocks is attributable to the pointed horn of the anvil that I keep handily mounted on a nearby billet.

The boar slept through it all.

I'm not sure why I did it, but after I doctored myself up with first aid and coffee, I spent the rest of the morning tidying up the pigs' stalls. In the course of cleaning troughs and lugging in fresh water, the boar came round, and I took unbecoming satisfaction from his glazed look and the way he was careful to set each trotter down.

As I worked, the sows snuffled my legs, nibbled at my rubber boots, and generally made quiet, contented sounds. When I finished mucking out the area, I spread one shovelful of sweet-smelling cedar sawdust across the pen, and that was a signal to them to begin cavorting.

Sawdust has a curious effect on pigs. It's almost as though it was the confetti of a celebration. I spread another, and the sows squealed, tossed their heads delightedly under the downfall, shivered ecstatically, and began to run higgeldy-piggeldy around the ten-by-ten pen. The more I threw in, the sillier they became. Next door, the boar groaned in self-pity.

When there was nothing more to be done, I leaned on the fence between the two stalls and watched as the sows nuzzled through the sawdust, nibbling on an occasional chip. The boar was recovering, but I knew with certainty that he was thinking he would never again be the pig he was before. Soberly I realized that *he* was right.

"Today's the day," I said aloud. All three of them stopped long enough to regard me with their uncannily human eyes. In their cold blue depths I imagined I saw comprehension . . . sadness . . . forgiveness?

With these bleak thoughts it was apropos that Harley Black chose that moment to pull into the dooryard.

"You the feller's got three pigs to boocher?" he asked as I met him in front of the barn.

Having always hauled our pigs to be slaughtered, I had never met the man before. I took him in. The first thing that struck me was that he wore the filthiest pair of coveralls I had ever seen. Unaccountably, I found myself slipping into the rural idiom. "Yup," I replied shortly.

"Yore name Swen . . . Swenky?"

"Near enough," I responded tersely. He hadn't shaved in a week, and the stubble under his chin was a sickly yellow from dribbled tobacco juice. A beetle-browed boy got out of the other side of the pickup and stood listlessly leaning against the truck's sideboards. He was nearly as filthy as his employer.

"Wet mornin'," Black observed.

"Yup."

He reached into the bib pocket of his coveralls and took out the wrinkled remains of a bag of Big Chief chewing tobacco. His dark, flat eyes took in everything about our stone house and the neat stone barn as he pinched a hen's-egg-sized wad of tobacco and tucked it into his right cheek.

"I get fifteen dollars a pig," he mumbled as he tossed the depleted bag to his young assistant.

It was the same price I had paid in the past, and that was after having endured the ordeal of loading and transporting the animals. On the face of it, it was a good deal. Nevertheless, I was beginning to feel some uncomfortable elitist reservations, not to mention some that turned around basic health considerations.

"Okay," I answered tersely.

"I reckon we better look at the job." He started toward the barn, and I nearly gagged as the ripe aroma of the professional slaughterer swept past me.

What Black and his helper may have lacked in personal hygiene, they made up for in professional competence. In minutes, Black found a suitable beam in the barn from which to suspend his spreading yard, and the boy unloaded the scalding tub. Without asking, he filled it with water from the barn faucet. Together they unloaded a rickety wooden table which they nestled up to the tub. Next came a large, hand-forged hook, a meat saw, and a communal wood scabbard holding efficient-looking knives and a sharpening steel. Finally, they wrestled a large pressurized gas container from the pickup and hooked it up so that a foot long flame played on the bottom of the tub. Not a word passed between them as they went about their work. They seemed oblivious to my brooding presence.

"Where're the pigs?" Black's back was to me as he

fumbled with something in the cab of his truck. The question startled me. A scant fifteen minutes had passed since they had pulled into the dooryard. Black turned, and he held a revolver in one hand and a knife in the other.

"Th . . . they're over here," I stammered, pointing in the direction of the two stalls around the corner. There was an irremedial lag between my brain and my tongue. Images were bouncing around my skull: little pigs emerging from a bran sack; adolescent pigs gambolling across an open field under a midsummer sun; grown hogs, become piglets again as they cavorted under the rain of sweet-smelling cedar sawdust.

"Umpf," grunted Black. He spat a stream of yellow juice. I followed in his ripe wake as he turned the corner.

It is a non sequitur to talk of death or love rationally. Once experienced, both defy description, and without experience, both are nonsense. Though it would be stoutly denied by most rural people, husbandry is a form of love (it is no accident that spouse is synonymous with husband), and the ultimate goal of all husbandry, be it of plant or animal, is to mourn the death of that which we nourished and loved. We call the wake a harvest celebration.

"Them two're good lookin' pigs," said Black when he came to a rest in front of the sows. "That'n," he pointed to the boar, "looks a mite peaked." In the sleety rain his flat black eyes seem to have taken on a sheen that matched the cold metal of his revolver. "Nawthin' pers'nal, but you don't look so hot yourself."

"Yeah," I replied lethargically.

He looked at me sharply. "You wanna go outside the barn while I . . ."

"No!" The vehemence of my response surprised me. Then more softly, "No, I reckon I'll stay."

He shrugged, and opened the door to the sows' stall.

I forced myself to watch as he carefully lined the muzzle up between a sow's eyes. "Bang!" The sow's legs flew out from under her, and there wasn't a tremor as she died. Deftly Black drew the sharp blade across her throat, and the blood pulsed across the clean, fresh sawdust. "Bang!" went the revolver again. Black didn't waste any motions.

The smell of the fresh blood was everywhere, and despite my resolve, I pulled back. A grunt from the next stall made me turn, and I found the boar's bloodshot eyes fixed on mine.

Black emerged from the sows' stall and started to open the door to the boar's.

I put my hand on the latch. "Do you mind," I asked in as even a voice as I could manage, "if I . . . kill . . . this one?"

He shifted the quid in his cheek as he stared at me flatly. "No, I reckon not."

"Hold on a minute," I said over my shoulder, "I'll be right back." I started toward the house.

I was back a minute later, and Black and the boy stared bemused at the two bottles of homemade beer I carried.

"Drinking buddy," I explained shortly. I took Slack's revolver in one hand and the beer in the other as I entered the pen and kicked the door shut behind me.

When I came out again five minutes later I carried the two empty bottles and the smoking gun. I did not try to hide the tears in my eyes.

Aloud I said, "The damned fool thought he was immortal." Inwardly I was thinking, "but illusion is just about all we've got left."

Cover and interior design by Julia Rowe
Typeset in Garamond Antiqua
  by Whitman Press
Printed on Glatfelter, an acid-free paper,
  by McNaughton & Gunn